Blade has just landed on the planet Targa and has quickly assessed the situation: He'd seldom met people in any Dimension who had so quickly convinced him he wasn't going to be on their side.

Blade was considering what to do next when the problem was solved. One of the dozen or so Targan soldiers whom he had been watching at a safe distance bent over a woman, opened his canteen, and emptied it onto her face. She twitched, gasped, choked, and tried feebly to sit up. Four other soldiers grabbed her arms and legs and began ripping off her clothes.

Blade watched, disgusted, but also noted the strange details revealed as the woman was stripped. She was totally unlike the soldiers. Her complexion was reddish brown; theirs was fair. She had long flowing hair of a silver cast, her limbs were long—she was as slender as any woman Blade had ever seen. She was sensual, yet ethereal.

Blade waited, trying not to hold his breath. Then the woman screamed, as one of the soldiers crawled on top of her and gave a grunting cry. Two sentries turned to watch the show and Blade knew what had to be done next. . . .

THE BLADE SERIES:

HEROIC FANTASY SERIES

29

An incredible time-space journey to Dimension X!

RICHARD BLADE

TREASURE OF THE STARS

by Jeffrey Lord

PINNACLE BOOKS • **LOS ANGELES**

This is a work of fiction. All the characters and events portrayed in this book are fictional, and any resemblance to real people or incidents is purely coincidental.

BLADE #29: TREASURE OF THE STARS

An original Pinnacle Books edition, published for the first time anywhere.

Produced by Lyle Kenyon Engel

First printing, November 1978

ISBN: 0-523-40207-4

Cover illustration by John Alvin

Printed in the United States of America

PINNACLE BOOKS, INC.
2029 Century Park East
Los Angeles, California 90067

TREASURE OF THE STARS

Chapter 1

The big man on the branch watched the soldiers passing thirty feet below. He watched them as intently as a hawk picking out its prey. None of the soldiers looked up or even seemed to realize there was such a direction. They tramped through the ankle-high grass, crackling twigs underfoot and ploughing through bushes. They made so much noise that the man in the tree could have followed their progress on a pitch-black night. If it weren't for the ugly-looking rifles in their hands, the soldiers would have been almost funny.

The man in the tree was armed only with a rough club and a rawhide sling. He wore only a barbaric collection of animal skins. No one would have laughed at him, though.

He was an inch over six feet tall, and weighed more than two hundred pounds. His heavy-boned frame was layered with superbly-conditioned muscles. His skin was darkened by wind, weather, sun, and dirt, and seamed with scars in at least a dozen places.

The last of the soldiers was passing under the tree and heading off downhill. Their eyes were still fixed on the ground or on the backs of their comrades. The man in the tree mentally noted other details about the soldiers besides their clumsiness and carelessness. They wore round black helmets with narrow white crests, dark green jackets and trousers that looked more elegant than comfortable, black leather boots and belts, dark brown packs on polished metal pack frames. Two men carried fat snub-nosed weapons that looked like giant shotguns—probably grenade launchers. The rest carried heavy rifles with big pan-shaped magazines, fixed bayonets, and elaborate sights. Each rifleman also had three or four egg-shaped red grenades hooked to his belt. One man carried a shiny long-barreled pistol.

1

The soldiers might be overdressed and clumsy, but they looked remarkably well-armed. If they could use their weapons better than they marched, they would be formidable.

So the man waited until the soldiers were well out of sight before climbing down from the tree. He stood for a moment at its base, listening carefully. The soldiers were still moving as noisily as ever. He could follow them without any trouble. He swung the club in his right hand and set off on the trail of the soldiers.

He moved with grace and power, putting his feet down with great precision yet still covering ground quickly. Every movement suggested the flawless coordination and reflexes of some powerful animal. Yet the heavy-boned dark face was too alive and aware to be an animal's, and the dark eyes were searching, restless, almost frighteningly intelligent. In this man, mind and body had joined to create a superb fighting machine, one that didn't seem to belong in the same world with those clumsy soldiers in green.

In fact, the man wasn't from the same world as the soldiers he followed. His name Was Richard Blade, this was Dimension X, and he'd come across infinity by what might be called science but still seemed more like a miracle.

Richard Blade actually didn't belong in his own homeland, modern Britain, much more than in Dimension X. He was a man whose mind and body were made for the lonely, dangerous, and frequently short life of the professional adventurer. He would have been a tower of strength to Francis Drake raiding Spanish galleons in the sixteenth century. In the safe, sanitary, ordered life of a modern industrial country, he was a man out of place.

Every so often, though, even the most oddly-shaped peg will find a suitable hole. When Blade left Oxford, a man called J was head of the secret intelligence agency MI6. He suspected what skills this young man might have, and made him a field agent straight out of the university. Blade justified J's confidence by becoming MI6's best field man. Time after time he succeeded in assignments which would have been suicidal for any other agent. He still knew he had nine chances out of ten of dying violently, but accepted this with open eyes. It was part of the price

2

to be paid for doing his duty and living a life which so well suited him.

Years passed, and in a laboratory under the Tower of London an aging, half-crippled, hunchbacked scientific genius conceived an experiment. His name was Lord Leighton, he was even more brilliant than he was eccentric, and the experiment was to link a sophisticated computer and a powerful human mind, then see what happened. He hoped to create a combined human-electronic intelligence with the virtues of both and the limitations of neither.

The human mind had to be powerful, and it had to be housed in an equally powerful body. So it was hardly surprising that Lord Leighton ended up with Richard Blade as his test subject. Blade was very nearly the best living example of the ancient ideal of "a sound mind in a sound body."

What happened after that surprised even Lord Leighton. The computer did not link itself with Blade's mind. Instead it twisted all of Blade's senses, so that he awoke to live and move about in a strange savage world called Alb. It was a world that might have existed thousands of years in Earth's past, but it was not really Earth. It was—Dimension X.

Blade faced all the dangers of Alb with the same skill and determination he'd used against enemy agents. Once more he survived, until Lord Leighton adjusted the computer, restored Blade's senses to normal, and brought him home to Britain.

Blade came home to a crisis. Obviously a whole new world lay out there in Dimension X, perhaps many worlds. If these worlds could be explored and exploited, there could be a new dawn and a new empire for Britain.

Just as obviously, the existence of Dimension X had to be kept secret. If it was revealed, no one knew for certain what might happen, but everybody expected the worst. Revealing the secret of Dimension X might lead to a nuclear war and the end of this world, rather than the discovery of new ones.

So Blade found himself caught up in the most vital topsecret project in British history. Lord Leighton continued as scientific head of Project Dimension X, producing larger and larger computers. A staff of hand-picked security-cleared technicians helped him as much as he would let them.

J added handling the security of the Project to his other duties. Less formally, he kept an eye on Blade, heading off Lord Leighton's wilder schemes when they threatened to put Blade in danger for no good reason. J was nearer seventy than sixty, a man nearing the end of his life, a man who'd been married to his duties all that life. Blade was the son he'd never had.

Inevitably, money was needed to expand and continue the Project, money by the millions of pounds, which had to be found somewhere. The Prime Minister's Secret Fund helped, and so did selling what Blade carried back from Dimension X—gold and jewels, strange drugs, stranger metals, the secrets of advanced technologies. Project Dimension X never got rich, never even showed a clear profit, but somehow kept going.

Blade made trip after trip into Dimension X, and little by little some of the mysteries vanished. No one could call the Project a failure, yet somehow the big successes everyone hoped for continued to be just out of reach.

None of the technological secrets Blade brought home could be exploited without years of expensive research and development.

There was no way to predict where Blade would end up, when Lord Leighton pulled the master switch on the computer. He'd visited some Dimensions more than once, but usually he entered a new world on each trip. Dimension X could never be explored or exploited this way.

Finally, the strain of travel from one Dimension to another was beyond most people's endurance. No one ever came back from Dimension X with Blade and stayed alive and sane for more than a few hours. No one except Blade had ever made the round trip from Home Dimension and stayed alive and sane at all. They'd been looking for another person with Blade's qualities for a long time, without finding one.

So the Project rested entirely on Blade's survival, and was horribly vulnerable because of this. In Dimension X Blade faced dangers that made anything in Home Dimension seem like children's games. He survived them all, but

4

the luck of even the most unkillable man will run out sooner or later.

Blade knew this, hoped for someone else to take over his job, but didn't let the matter worry him. He had to keep going as long as he could. It was a matter of duty, and more than that.

Blade thrived on the life of a secret agent, but it wasn't a completely free life. He was always part of an organization, even if the rest of it was thousands of miles away. He was always operating under rules and restraints, and he was always operating in a twentieth-century world. In Dimension X he was a man alone, nothing between him and a gruesome death but his own skill, strength, and wits.

More time passed, and one morning Richard Blade went through a familiar routine for the twenty-ninth time. He went to the Tower of London and was identified by grim-faced Special Branch men guarding the entrance to the underground complex. He took an elevator two hundred feet down to the complex, then walked a long echoing corridor, guarded by a score of electronic sentinels.

At the door of the computer section J met him, a little grayer than before, perhaps, but still as erect as a sword and quietly concerned about Blade. Together they passed through the rooms full of supporting equipment and entered the main computer room.

There Lord Leighton waited for them, among the towering gray crackle-finished consoles of his great computer. Blade went into a small room carved in the rock wall and prepared himself for his trip. He stripped naked, smeared himself with foul-smelling black grease to prevent electrical burns, and pulled on a loincloth.

Then he came back out into the main room and sat down in a rubber-padded chair standing in a glass booth in the middle of the computer's consoles. J watched as Leighton scurried around Blade, attaching cobra-headed metal electrodes to every part of Blade's body—ears, fingers, toes, even his penis. From each electrode a colored wire trailed off into the computer.

Meanwhile Blade hyperventilated, to fill his system with oxygen. Slowly he felt the tension flow out of him to be replaced by an eager anticipation of what he might find in Dimension X this time.

Leighton finished his work and gave it a final inspection.

He walked to the main control panel and watched the master timer as the computer readied itself for the great moment.

Then J raised a hand in a farewell salute, Lord Leighton's hand came down on the red master switch, and Blade whirled off into Dimension X.

Chapter 2

Most of the time Blade traveled from Home Dimension to Dimension X in an explosive psychedelic bombardment of all his senses. Sometimes it was merely spectacular, sometimes terrifying, sometimes agonizingly painful.

This time there was nothing like that. The computer room and everything in it vanished. In its place was an endless blackness, with silver and golden lights twinkling starlike in a thousand places. Blade felt hints of a terrible cold all around him, felt his skin beginning to prickle—then blackness and all the other sensations vanished. A moment in limbo, then a bone-jarring thud as he landed on a solid surface which seemed to be covered with some sort of padding.

Blade kept his eyes closed and listened for any sounds that could mean immediate danger. He heard the sighing of wind, the creak of branches, and the twitters and chirps of several kinds of birds. Nothing else.

Blade continued to lie still while he counted to twenty, allowing his body to reorient itself. His head ached slightly, but no worse than it would have done from a mild sinus attack. He felt none of the blinding agony which sometimes used to leave him immobile and vulnerable for half an hour. The hyperventilating seemed to prevent that sort of headache.

Blade opened his eyes and sat up. He was sitting as naked as the day he was born on a thick layer of fallen blue needles. He seemed to be on a wooded hillside, surrounded by large trees. Some carried the blue needles and soared up out of sight, while other squatter ones spread wide and trailed long golden leaves. The ground was nearly clear except for fallen needles and occasional patches of waist-high reddish ferns. Upslope Blade caught a glimpse of blue sky and drifting white clouds. He listened again for any sounds except wind and birds, again heard nothing, and headed up the hill.

The top of the hill was farther than he'd expected. He covered at least a mile before he broke out of the trees onto open, rocky ground. A few yards in front of him the ground dropped sharply away into a rugged cliff. Several hundred feet below it ended on the bank of a twisting little river, clear blue where it flowed deep, silvery where it boiled through a stretch of rapids. On the other side of the river the forest began again, an endless carpet of blue and gold with smaller patches of red. Blade had seldom seen such a lush and colorful display of vegetation outside the tropics.

Many miles away across the treetops, the ground swelled into a range of green hills, then abruptly leaped upward into a wall of mountains. The sunlight blazed off snowscapes and glaciers twisting down scarred rocky flanks. Blade could only guess how high the mountains rose, but they looked at least as high as the Alps. They cut off the horizon in all directions except for one narrow valley.

The sky was blue, with faint brownish-gray tinge. Blade sniffed the air. It was brisk and clean, the air of a virgin wilderness a thousand miles from civilization. Whatever tinged the sky didn't seem to be affecting the air.

With a brisk wind blowing, it was almost chilly in the open. From the position of the sun Blade guessed it was early afternoon. He decided to get under cover or at least out of the wind before nightfall. Up here night could be dangerously chilly for a naked man.

Blade began prowling along the cliff, looking for a way down. Along the river he'd be out of the wind, and he'd have drinking water and possibly fish. The river might even give him a trail out of this wilderness to whatever civilization this Dimension might have.

Blade had never landed in a totally uninhabited Dimension and didn't really want to. A Dimension with no intelligent inhabitants might be useful for colonization, but that would need larger-scale transportation into Dimension X. It wouldn't be very useful for Richard Blade, who would have to survive like an animal, with nothing but his bare hands and his wits. There was such a thing as being too alone!

The shadows were getting long before Blade found a place where the cliff had crumbled away to a slope. A stream breaking out of the fallen rocks made them dark and slick, but he'd climbed barehanded under worse conditions before. With a final look at the forest, he lowered himself onto the upper end of the rockfall and began working his way down.

The way down was longer and harder than Blade expected. Several times he had to jump down farther than he liked, landing precariously and picking up a growing collection of bruises. Once he slipped, rolled thirty feet downward, nearly sprained his wrist, and came to a stop just short of a vertical drop onto sharp rocks. It was twilight before he reached the bottom of the rockfall.

In front of him the river swept past the rocks so fast Blade realized it would be suicide to try swimming across here. He moved on downstream, exploring the riverbank.

He was just about resigned to spending the night curled up among the rocks when his luck turned. Beyond a line of boulders, the river formed a broad, dark pool, deep and slow-moving. Blade plunged straight in.

The water was icy cold, but after the first shock Blade found it refreshing. It scoured away some of the grime and sweat, eased the aches and pains, and left him feeling a great deal better.

His feet were just touching bottom on the far side of the river when a hissing scream sounded high overhead. Blade dove forward, getting underwater without making a splash. Then he poked his head above the surface, just as the scream came again, three times in rapid succession.

Looking up, Blade saw a weird shape sail across the sky. It reminded him of a slim mountain lion with tufted ears and long clawed legs. Heavy ribbed membranes like bat wings extended between the legs, giving enough lifting surface to support the beast in the air. The creature glided across the sky like an immense flying squirrel, steering with its short flat tail.

Blade counted nine more of the bat-cats before the last one disappeared. He faintly heard more screams from well upstream, where they seemed to have landed, then growling which slowly faded away. It sounded as if the beasts were feeding. On what, Blade didn't know, but knew he'd better be careful or the next time it might be on him. The bat-cats were large enough to be dangerous opponents for an unarmed man, even if they hadn't hunted in packs.

Blade headed downstream again, staying in the water for a few hundred yards to avoid leaving a trail. Then he climbed out of the water, exercised vigorously to warm himself up and unkink his muscles, and kept going.

The sun went down in an awesome display of orange, purple, and red which seemed to cover half the sky. Blade kept moving until the light was nearly gone and even his superb night vision could barely make out the ground in front of him. Then he found a narrow V between two roots of a large tree, drifted full of dead leaves. He crept in on hands and knees, settled himself with his back against the trunk, and piled over his legs and stomach all the leaves he could reach.

It wasn't much protection, and he could only hope that none of the bat-cats would come by while he slept. It was still better than stumbling on through the night, more tired and chilled with each mile.

Blade slid lower into the leaves, piled more over his chest, then lay back to sleep.

Blade awoke when the sky was still a dirty gray, as a familiar sound blasted across the forest and jerked him out of sleep. It was the roar of a low-flying jet plane.

Blade sprang to his feet, wide awake and looking around for the nearest spot where he could see the sky. A quick look told him there wasn't any nearer than the riverbank. He dashed down the slope, narrowly missing trees, leaping over stumps and fallen logs, reaching the open just as the sound of the jet faded away to the south.

Before he could draw in enough breath to curse, he heard more jets approaching from the north. He had time to step back into the trees far enough to see without being seen. Then the jets raced overhead less than a thousand feet up. They were flying slowly enough to give Blade a good view of them.

He'd heard of drawing-board projects like these jets, but he'd never seen or heard of anything like them getting off the ground anywhere in Home Dimension. The fuselages were disk-shaped, flattened and nearly as wide as they were long. Twin rudders jutted up from the rear of the disk, and on either side projected short swept-back wings.

A pair of jet engines was sunk into the root of each wing and a cluster of gray cylinders looking unpleasantly like bombs hung from a rack near each wingtip. The undersides of the planes were blue-gray and the tops camouflaged in blobs and stripes of green and brown. There was some sort of insignia on the wings, but the planes were gone before Blade could make it out.

The whistle and roar of the jets died away. Blade walked a little farther under the cover of the trees before sitting down to think. He didn't want to run any risk of being spotted now. If those gray cylinders were really bombs, each plane was carrying enough to demolish a good stretch of forest if they thought he was a suitable target.

He wished he'd been able to make out the insignia on the planes. It would have answered one awkward question. Those jets looked odd, but they were at about the same technological level as Home Dimension. Blade knew only one world in Dimension X where this was so—the strange world where an other-England called the Empire of Englor fought an other-Russia called Russland. Was he back in that Dimension, one of the weirdest and deadliest he'd ever visited?

If he was, he might have a problem. The presence of the jets suggested he was in territory ruled by one or the other of the two great powers. There was no wilderness like this anywhere in Englor or any of its allies, as far as he knew. Was he in Russland or some Russland satellite?

If he was, he was in danger. The rulers of Russland were an iron-fisted military elite called the Red Flames. Their policy toward strangers was shoot on sight—unless they wanted to ask a few questions, in which case the stranger was better off being shot. If he was in Russland, by some quirk of the computer or the unknown forces governing Dimension X, he might actually be better off playing Tarzan in the wilderness until the time came for him to return home.

However, three mysterious jet planes did not make a Russland. Blade laughed at his own overactive imagination. He couldn't afford to spend too much time worrying about unanswerable questions. This Dimension had a civilization, that civilization was technologically advanced,

11

and he was going to find it. He was also going to keep out of sight as much as possible on his way to find it.

That was enough for the moment. Blade found a branch lying on the ground, large enough and sound enough to make a good club. He shouldered it and set off, still heading downstream.

Chapter 3

For the next three days Blade tramped steadily downstream, never more than a hundred yards from the riverbank and never that far from the cover of the trees. He didn't risk a fire, but there was plenty of food to be eaten raw. He found berries, edible mushrooms, a small reddish fish, and something like a rabbit-sized squirrel with long floppy ears. None of them tasted very good, but together all of them kept him alive. After the second day he had enough skins from the squirrel-rabbits to make himself sandals and a loinguard.

The winged-disk jet planes passed low overhead at least once each day. Sometimes they carried the gray cylinders, at other times large yellow tanks. Twice Blade saw the vapor trails of other jets flying too high to be identified, and once he heard something that sounded vaguely like a helicopter. Once he heard a more ominous sound in the distance, a series of echoing roars like explosions.

On the fourth day Blade reached a point where the river broke through the foothills of the mountains, forming a rugged canyon. He had an all-day struggle to get through the canyon. Several times he ended up clinging by fingers and toes to sheer rock faces with long drops to the rapids below him. Both his grip and his luck held. By late afternoon he was out of the canyon, facing the wooded lowlands beyond.

A plane flew overhead as Blade made camp that night, lower than usual and cruising slowly so he was able to make out the insignia. The plane bore a green triangle with a red border and golden wings, not the insignia of the Russlanders or any of their allies. This was a new Dimension with a new, unknown people. Blade slept better that night than he'd done the first three nights, because of the good news and because it was warmer down here in the lowlands. Sandals and a fur loinguard didn't do much to keep off the night breezes.

He was on the move before dawn the next day. As it grew light he bathed and caught three fish for breakfast. An hour after breakfast he reached open ground. An hour farther on, much of the relief he'd felt at learning he wasn't in Russland suddenly vanished.

In front of him lay a crater, half a mile across, more than a hundred feet deep, outlines softened by erosion and long grass but quite unmistakable. Once, long ago, an atomic bomb had exploded here.

How long ago? The grass was thick and looked healthy enough, while bushes and even small trees grew on the very lip of the crater. Long enough for most of the radioactivity to be gone, it seemed.

Blade walked in a wide circle around the crater, finding bits of metal, black, twisted, half-melted, chunks of stone and concrete, blobs of glass, slabs of what might once have been a road leading down to the river. He couldn't even guess what might have stood here before the bomb. Whether or not it hit its intended target, it did a thorough job where it struck.

Blade wondered if the rest of the bombs that must have gone off in that long-ago war had done an equally thorough job. Probably not—this civilization still had enough sophisticated jet planes to fly them over this wilderness every day. However much they'd mangled themselves, they weren't a bunch of cavemen.

What else were they? Blade wondered as he made his way across the open ground. He kept low, his eyes searching the sky, ready to dive under the nearest bush or into the nearest patch of long grass at the first sound of a plane. The only way to find out more about these people was to push on until he met them, but he still didn't want to be spotted by one of the planes. It would be hard to prove he was friendly by waving at the pilot, and hard to survive if the pilot decided he was an enemy.

Blade left the open ground behind well before dark. The next day he found himself in the woods again. It was no longer virgin wilderness, but second growth on land which had once been farms. Every mile or so he passed traces of stone walls, farm buildings, bridges over streams, even a road. No traces of violence, though. Had nature covered them over, or hadn't there been any? Perhaps the people of the area simply packed up and left after the war, or perhaps they died from something that left their homes and walls intact. Radiation, disease, chemicals, starvation, radiation-induced sterility?

Blade found himself more and more reluctant to push on with no weapon but his rough club. He tore off a length of tough vine, then went down to the riverbank and picked out a handful of rounded stones, each about half the size of his fist. With a little practice he had a fairly useful sling. It might not slay Goliath, but he could hit a man in the head with one of the stones at twenty-five yards. After the stones were gone, the vine was tough enough to use as a strangling cord. Blade made a belt out of another length of vine and a pouch out of the hide of one of the squirrel-rabbits. Then he dropped the stones into the pouch and moved on.

If they could only work the bugs out of getting some equipment into Dimension X along with him! He wouldn't ask for much, just a few essentials like boots, a canteen, emergency rations, and some sort of weapon. He'd even be happy if the scientists would let go of his old commando knife, which had made the round trip with him. The scientists insisted they still needed it for further study, Lord Leighton supported them, and against that combination even J's protests couldn't do anything.

That evening the planes seemed to be coming overhead in squadrons. Blade was careful to get well under cover, and when he started off the next morning he moved more cautiously than before.

It was a good thing he did. Just before noon he saw nearly a dozen planes diving on something only a few miles ahead. Then he heard a steady crashing of explosions. After a few minutes the explosions died away, the planes flew off, and several new flying machines came whirring in over the treetops. They looked like immense gleaming sausages with lift propellers in the wings and drive propellers in their high tails. When one of them hovered, then landed a mile ahead, Blade decided to get out of sight. He was at the base of a tree when he heard the soldiers approaching. By the time they came in sight he was thirty feet up, hard to pick out even if they'd thought of looking.

When the soldiers passed, he still wasn't completely sure he ought to try meeting them. They looked as if they were on a combat mission, they might be rather trigger-happy, and if they were they were carrying enough firepower to make themselves thoroughly deadly to Richard Blade. Slings and clubs against automatic rifles wasn't his idea of safe odds.

However, these soldiers didn't seem to have much idea of how to handle themselves in the woods. He could almost certainly follow them anywhere, without having to meet them if he didn't want to.

So he climbed down the tree and set off on the trail of the soldiers.

The soldiers not only moved noisily, they moved slowly. Blade's main problem at first was not overtaking them and being seen. After a while he realized that wasn't going to be much of a problem either. The soldiers' training hadn't included *anything* about how to move cross-country in hostile territory. They marched looking mostly ahead, occasionally to the side, never above or behind.

Unless there was a second patrol following this one, guarding their rear? Blade thought he'd better check. He dropped back, hid under a bush, and waited, listening to the first patrol tramping off, then listening for the approach of a second.

Eventually he decided the first patrol really was being as careless as it looked and set off after them again. When he came in sight of them, they were still tramping along as casually as before. Some were beginning to sweat and most of the uniforms were no longer quite so crisp and clean. Otherwise they still looked as if they were parading in front of their own barracks. Blade began to wonder if this was just an exercise, where even the worst sort of carelessness would earn the soldiers nothing more than a chewing-out from some sergeant or officer.

He'd just completed the thought when there was a thunderous explosion not far ahead. Even through the treetops Blade could see a mountain of gray smoke towering against the sky. The ground heaved, birds screeched, small animals dashed about in terror, twigs, leaves, and birds' nests showered down on Blade. Most of the soldiers threw themselves on the ground.

16

A yellowish-brown animal the size of a small deer burst out of the undergrowth to Blade's right, plunging toward the line of soldiers. One of them rose on his elbows, aimed his rifle, and squeezed off a burst. Whatever the rifle fired, it hit hard enough to not only blow the animal's head off but cut down a couple of small trees behind it. The headless corpse collapsed, spouting blood, and the trees dropped on top of it.

Before the animal stopped twitching, the burst of rifle fire was echoed from ahead and to the left. Bursts alternated with single shots and the noise steadily increased. Blade heard grenade explosions, shouts, and once the unmistakable shrieks of someone in agony.

So much for the notion that he'd wandered into some harmless maneuvers! He began to wonder if the best thing might not be to wander out again while the soldiers were fighting their battle. He didn't see any particular point in getting his head blown off like the animal's.

Then suddenly running feet thudded and bushes crackled to the right of the soldiers. Five running figures burst out into the open. Four of them were men, one a woman with long pale silvery hair. All of them were carrying rifles or pistols.

Both sides were paralyzed with surprise for a moment. Then the paralysis ended and the forest exploded with a deafening roar of gunfire as both sides let fly. Blade flattened himself on the ground. For the moment he could tell what was happening without seeing it, and he didn't want to be drilled by any of the stray bullets whistling in all directions like mad bees.

A grenade went off, followed by several screams and the crash of a tree going over. Then more bursts, mixed with a few single shots, a sizzling sound, the woman's voice crying out something high-pitched and incoherent, and several men shouting what must have been curses. Finally there was silence, except for the gurgling and moaning of the wounded.

A few inches at a time, Blade crept to where he could get a better view of the scene. By the time he'd finished moving, the survivors were getting themselves sorted out.

The clearing looked like a crude slaughterhouse, with hacked carcasses lying about and blood everywhere. Blade counted eight of the soldiers either dead or so mangled he

17

hoped they were dead. Three men of the other side were also dead, and one was groaning with a bloody arm and shoulder. The woman was sprawled on her back, her clothes torn in a couple of places and her face smoke-blackened. Otherwise she seemed unhurt.

Some of the surviving soldiers were gathering up the undamaged weapons and ammunition from the bodies. Others, including the officer with the pistol, surrounded the enemy survivors. Blade saw the officer bend over the man.

"Your name?" As usual, the passage into Dimension X had altered Blade's brain so that the officer's language came to him as English.

A groan from the man.

The officer kicked the man in the ribs. He screamed.

"Your name?"

A wordless muttering. This time the officer kicked the man in the groin. He doubled up gasping, without the breath to scream.

"Your name, *you filthy wild swine!*"

This time the man said something Blade couldn't catch, but was obviously insulting: The officer's face twisted and turned dark. He gripped his pistol and squeezed the trigger. It was a laser, and the beam seared across the man's cheek, leaving a charred mark and destroying one eye. The officer fired several more times, until the man's face was a ruin of charred flesh and blackened bone. Then the officer signaled to one of the soldiers, who finished the man with a bayonet thrust in the ribs.

Blade found himself itching to have a gun in his hand and its sights on the officer. He'd seldom met people in any Dimension who'd so quickly convinced him he wasn't going to be on their side. He wasn't sure what side the soldiers' victims belonged to, but it had to be a better starting point for this Dimension than the soldiers!

He was considering what to do next when the problem was solved for him. One of the soldiers bent over the woman, opened his canteen, and emptied it onto her face. She twitched, gasped, choked, and tried feebly to sit up. Four other soldiers grabbed her arms and legs and began ripping off her clothes. Blade watched, disgusted but also noting strange details revealed as the woman was stripped.

Her skin was reddish-brown where it wasn't dark with smoke, dirt, and bruises. It was totally unlike the soldiers, who were mostly about Blade's complexion. Both the long hair on the woman's head and the tight triangle between her legs were white with a faint, barely visible silvery sheen.

She was long-limbed and so slender it was hard to detect the normal female curves in her body. Yet she didn't look starved or masculine. She was simply more slender than any human woman Blade had ever seen. There was an ethereal quality about her, like a fairy woman.

Then one of the soldiers jerked off the man's shirt the woman wore under her jacket, leaving her completely naked. This lifted one arm so that the hand was silhouetted in the air. Blade had a clear view of a hand with six long fingers on it, each finger with an extra joint.

Humanoid, Blade thought, *but definitely not human. No question of who to help.* Even if the soldiers hadn't behaved like sadistic thugs, this woman had to be helped. Blade needed to know who she was, where she came from, and what she was doing in this Dimension of otherwise normal human beings. To even ask her these questions, he'd have to get her out of the hands of the soldiers, and he couldn't see any way of doing that peacefully.

So now he knew what had to be done next. The question left was: how?

Chapter 4

Whatever Blade did, he'd have to do it quickly. He'd also have to get one of the rifles as fast as possible. The woman would probably be killed when the soldiers were finished with her, and tackling a dozen of even the clumsiest soldiers as he was would be suicide. Blade shifted to the left, where a stand of young trees offered better cover. He crawled on his belly like a snake, losing one sandal but hanging on to the pouch with the sling stones.

By the time Blade reached the trees a lively argument was going on among the soldiers. The officers wanted the woman kept alive for interrogation. Most of the soldiers wanted to pull down their pants and leap on her at once.

"We don't get one like her very often," said one, and his comrades muttered agreement.

"All right," the officer finally said. "If she won't talk, you can have her." He bent over the woman, took one wrist, and twisted just hard enough to make her face contort in pain.

"Your name, mudskin bitch! And what were you doing with the woodrats, anyway?"

The woman shook her head silently. The officer repeated the questions, got more silence, and twisted her wrist hard enough to make her cry out. The attempted interrogation went on for quite a while along those lines. The officer's face slowly darkened with rage and frustration, while the woman soon lost the breath to even scream.

"Hey, leave some life in her for us, for Mork's sake!" said one of the soldiers at last. The officer shrugged and stepped back.

"Well enough. She's yours. But let's not be foolish. Shturz, Hegen, Durgo—take up a triangle with the points *there*." He pointed at three soldiers, then at three points around the clearing. Blade saw that one of those points was right in front of the trees where he lay hidden, another off to his left.

The three soldiers took up their positions, while one of their comrades started opening his pants. The officer holstered his laser and stepped back. Blade crept backward until he was at the edge of the trees. Now he could no longer see the woman and the men around her clearly. He could still see both the sentry to his left and the one in front of the trees. That should be enough for now.

Blade waited, trying not to hold his breath. Then the woman screamed, the soldier on top of her gave a grunting cry, both sentries turned to watch the show, and Blade went into action.

He rose, dropping a stone into the sling and whirling it around his head faster and faster. The woman's cries drowned the hiss of the sling winding up for the throw. At the last moment the flicker of movement caught the first sentry's eye. He started to turn, Blade's arm snapped out, the stone flew from the sling and smashed into the soldier's forehead. He fell, not quite as spectacularly as Goliath, but with a satisfying thud.

As the first sentry hit the ground, Blade sprinted around the trees to attack the second. The third sentry on the far side of the clearing saw Blade and opened his mouth to shout. That was all he could do. His comrades were between him and Blade. If he'd fired at the Englishman he'd have massacred half of them.

The second sentry whirled as Blade came at him, thrusting with his bayonet. Blade sidestepped the thrust, gripped the rifle barrel with both hands, and jerked. The rifle came out of the soldier's hands like a cork out of a bottle. Blade smashed the butt into the sentry's throat, splintering the larynx into a hundred pieces. The man went over backward and writhed on the ground, hands clawing at his throat for the air it would no longer take in.

Blade threw himself on the ground almost at the foot of the dying man. He flipped off the rifle's safety and raised the muzzle, aiming well above the woman on the ground. At this range he could hardly miss such a fat target, even with an unfamiliar weapon.

He squeezed the trigger and the rifle bucked and quivered, spewing rounds with a hammering metallic roar. The only soldier who reacted fast enough was the officer.

21

He threw himself on the ground as the burst slashed through the men around him. They went down in a heap, screaming and writhing, blood and torn flesh and chopped-off arms and legs flying into the air from the impact of the bullets. By the time Blade stopped firing, the only soldiers left in shape to fight were the officer and the man on top of the woman.

The officer jumped up, drawing his laser. Blade swung the rifle toward him, squeezing the trigger again. The rifle hammered in a quick burst, then clicked empty. The officer fell but was still alive. He raised his laser as Blade reached into his pouch for another stone and threw. The stone cracked into the officer's cheek as he fired. The laser beam passed close enough to Blade to singe hair and one ear, then went on to crisp leaves and blacken bark on the trees behind him. Blade jumped up, moving faster than the dying officer could follow him with the laser's muzzle, closed, and rammed his bayonet into the man's throat.

By this time the soldier on top of the woman, in spite of his lust, had realized something was badly wrong. He was raising himself on his arms as Blade loomed over him. He looked up, lust and ox-like stupidity giving way to fear on his broad face, as Blade raised his rifle. At the last moment Blade remembered a bayonet thrust might go right through the soldier and hit the woman, so he reversed the rifle and struck with the butt. It crashed into the base of the soldier's skull, breaking his neck and slamming him forward onto the woman so hard she screamed again.

Blade put down the rifle, heaved the dead body off the woman, and bent over her. She was barely conscious, with bruises between her thighs, a cut lip, and a long shallow gouge across one shoulder. Her eyes were glazed and her breath was coming in quick, shallow gasps.

Blade unhooked his last victim's canteen and put it on the ground within the woman's reach. Then he picked up the man's rifle and switched its magazine to his own. Finally he began pulling off the soldier's clothes and putting them on.

The dead soldier was shorter than Blade but nearly as heavy-framed, so his clothes more or less fit. Even the helmet went on comfortably enough. When he'd finished, Blade wouldn't have won any Best-Dressed Man awards, but he did look much less like a caveman.

By the time Blade was dresssed, the woman was sitting up and holding the canteen to her lips with one hand. With the other hand she was feeling her body for serious injuries. While the woman examined herself, Blade walked over to the sentry he'd killed with the sling. His uniform seemed to be the only other one still wearable. All the rest were blood-drenched or dismembered along with the soldiers who'd been wearing them. Blade stripped off the man's clothes and brought them back to the woman.

By then she was washing her face in the last of the water from the canteen. She looked up at Blade, the glazed look gone but her face still showing doubt and confusion. Blade didn't blame her. She was as much at his mercy as she'd been at the soldiers', and he looked far more like them than like her.

Blade smiled. "Don't worry. I'm a friend, or at least no friend to those—!" He jerked a thumb at the corpses of the soldiers. "My name is Blade. Who are you and where—?"

He broke off as he noticed the woman was staring at him blank-faced, as if she didn't understand a word he was saying. The moment he stopped she began speaking a stream of quick, high-pitched one and two-syllable words. At least they sounded like words—Blade couldn't be sure. He suspected from the woman's tone that she was nervous, frightened, and trying to get an urgent message across to him. He might have guessed most of that if she'd never opened her mouth!

Again Blade asked, "Who are you?" and again the woman might as well have replied in Mandarin Chinese for all Blade could understand her. They went through this exchange twice more, as an unpleasant fact slowly dawned on Blade.

The strange twisting of his brain which made him understand and speak the language in each new Dimension wasn't working here. He could understand the soldiers, and no doubt they'd understand him if he ever had to talk to them. It was different with the woman. His own words were coming out in English, and the woman's in her own language, whatever that was.

Blade laughed—briefly. The situation was ludicrous, and it wasn't entirely surprising. This woman was of another race than the soldiers, a race not entirely human.

23

Why should she necessarily speak the soldiers' language merely because Blade's brain could now handle it?

The situation was also dangerous. He and the woman were facing a desperate flight for their lives without being able to understand a single word from each other. This wouldn't be completely impossible, but there were easier ways to manage it.

Well, let's start somewhere, he thought. Sign language certainly wouldn't do any harm. He pointed at himself and said very slowly, "Richard Blade."

The woman nodded, managed a faint smile, and pointed at herself. "Riyannah."

Blade smiled, then pointed at the forest around them with what he hoped would be an inquiring look on his face. They had to get out of here as fast as they could, and he wanted her advice on the best route.

He had to repeat the gesture three times. Then Riyannah nodded and pointed at the bushes behind her. Blade matched her gesture and her smile broadened. So they were to retrace the path she and her dead comrades had followed? Well, the bushes would certainly hide them from any more soldiers.

Riyannah didn't need Blade's gesture to start pulling on the clothes he'd brought for her. She winced at nearly every movement and couldn't always hold back a gasp of pain. Blade decided he'd do some first aid on her as soon as they could risk stopping. Riyannah might not have any serious injuries, but she was certainly bruised, battered, and probably on the edge of shock. He found another canteen with water in it and handed it to Riyannah, then started scavenging the battlefield for useful gear.

He collected as much as he thought he could carry, then pulled on the loaded pack. By the time he'd finished getting ready to move out, Riyannah was nearly dressed. She'd managed to salvage her own boots, and was slinging on a rifle, ammunition pouches, and a small rucksack of her own.

Blade touched a bruise on her cheek just below one ear, then tapped the rifle and shook his head. Riyannah shook her head even more violently, pantomimed raising a rifle and firing it, then held up two fingers. The message was clear: I can handle the load, and two rifles will be better than one.

Blade smiled and rested both hands lightly on her shoulders for a moment. He would have embraced her if she hadn't been so bruised and sore. He couldn't understand a word she said, but he could understand courage and common sense without any words.

They turned and headed into the bushes. Insects were already settling on the dead men behind them.

Chapter 5

The tangle of bushes and young trees stretched for several miles. No one could have seen Blade and Riyannah from the air, or for more than twenty feet away on the ground. As for trailing them—certainly not these soldiers!

Riyannah was obviously not much more at home in the woods than the soldiers. Her feet caught in roots, snapped twigs, sometimes got tangled up enough to bring her to her knees. Somehow she always got to her feet again and kept on going. Sweat poured down her face, her hair became a sodden, tangled mess, blood trickled from thorn scratches on her hands, a stone left an ugly mark on one knee. Blade helped her whenever he could, but half the time she shook off his hands. Pride, or didn't she trust him?

Whatever was driving Riyannah, it kept her going until they'd left the underbrush behind them. A stream flowed past the fringes of the brush. They stopped and refilled their canteens, then Riyannah pointed off to the right and put a finger to her lips. Blade nodded and they moved off again, this time doing their best to move silently as well as stay under cover.

Less than a mile farther, on they came to another clearing at the foot of a hill. The clearing was now a good deal larger than it had been and the hill somewhat smaller. The cause of both changes was clearly visible beyond a fringe of blown-down trees—a crater in the hillside, a hundred feet wide and a third that deep. The hillside, the clearing, and the trees for half a mile around the crater were littered with bodies, parts of bodies, smashed guns, flattened helmets, and bits of metal, leather, and cloth which might have been anything.

Blade counted three of the propeller-driven flying troop carriers in sight. One lay broken into three twisted and

26

blackened pieces, on top of a pile of trees turned into charcoal by burning fuel. From it Blade caught the too-familiar stench of freshly-roasted human flesh.

The second carrier lay at the foot of the hill just beyond the trees, tipped on its side, one stubby wing crushed out of shape and the cockpit a shambles of blood, twisted controls, and powdered glass. Several blanket-wrapped bodies lay on the grass beside it.

The third machine stood safely on top of the hill, soldiers standing almost shoulder to shoulder around it. Blade made out two large guns mounted on tripods and something else which looked like a rocket launcher. As he watched, a fourth troop carrier floated in to land on the hilltop and started pouring out more soldiers. Some of them joined their comrades, while others unfolded stretchers and began making their way down the hill toward the two wrecks.

Blade looked at Riyannah. Tears were running down her cheeks, making trails in the dirt. She was biting her lip to keep from sobbing out loud, and both hands were gripping a fallen branch so tightly her knuckles were white. She kept looking at the rifle on the ground beside her, then at Blade, then shaking her head. Each time she did that, the tears seemed to come faster.

It wasn't hard for Blade to understand the situation and what Riyannah was feeling. There'd been a base of some sort here, for people fighting the soldiers. The soldiers attacked the base, and somehow it blew up. That was the explosion Blade heard and saw. Most of the people in the base died in the blast or were killed by the soldiers. Riyannah and a few of her comrades escaped, only to be caught as they fled through the forest.

So no wonder Riyannah was weeping. Her cause, whatever it was, had taken a costly defeat. Dozens of her friends and comrades lay dead in the forest or buried under tons of earth and rock. The soldiers had taken heavy losses, but there were still too many of them around, alive and with guns in their hands. All Riyannah could hope to do was crawl away, leaving the soldiers crawling over the wreckage of the base like maggots, and hope to win her vengeance some other time.

Blade suspected she'd have his help when that time came. He wished he could be sure, but there were still too

27

many unanswered questions. Who were the soldiers, who were her friends, and what were the two sides fighting over? How many of Riyannah's friends were human, and how many were of her race? There were a dozen more questions, all of them needing answers. Like Riyannah's vengeance, they'd have to wait. There was nothing more either he or Riyannah could do here.

Blade pointed at the forest and looked at Riyannah. She nodded and pointed to the north. Biting back a groan, she heaved herself to her feet, and Blade followed her.

As they left the clearing behind, three jets went over, so high they were only metallic gleams at the heads of white vapor trails. As the forest swallowed up Blade again, he heard another jet, this one flying low.

They headed north for several hours. The trees began to thin out and it became harder to keep under cover. Several times Blade tried to suggest to Riyannah that they should use another, more protected route to wherever she wanted to go. Each time she merely shook her head and kept going. Either Blade's sign language wasn't getting through to her, or she was determined to get where she was going as quickly as possible.

Eventually they stopped to rest, under cover of a clump of bushes that reminded Blade of giant tulips with spiky blue leaves. They had to stop, because Riyannah was beginning to stagger with fatigue at almost every step. She lay quietly, eyes staring blankly at the sky, gasping for breath, while Blade washed her face and massaged some of the worst kinks out of her muscles.

Blade rummaged through his pack until he found the salvaged emergency rations. They were plastic-wrapped reddish-brown bars, and tasted about as Blade expected. Somewhere in the universe there might be a maker of emergency rations with a sense of taste, but so far Blade hadn't run into one. These bars tasted like laundry soap mixed with shellac.

They did quiet his rumbling stomach and give him some fresh energy. Riyannah was too exhausted to eat more than half of one bar, but it seemed to help her also. After another drink of water she was able to get to her feet and continue the march.

By now it was mid-afternoon. Before too much longer

they should start looking for a place with water and plenty of cover, to spend the night. Blade wondered if he could get this message through to Riyannah. The woman looked determined enough to march to the end of the world, if her legs held out that long.

They made a detour to the east down a long, heavily wooded slope. By the time they came out of the trees at the bottom the sky to the west was beginning to turn red. Across a shallow river lay a range of hills, with a broad valley opening toward Blade and Riyannah.

Blade sat down and pulled off his boots to massage his feet. The scavenged boots weren't quite a perfect fit. He was going to have blisters on his blisters if this march lasted more than a few days. For the tenth time he considered trying to ask Riyannah where they were going, and for the tenth time decided it was impossible. The question simply involved too many ideas no one could handle in sign language.

He was taking off his left boot when he saw light gleaming on metal, far off in the sky over the hills. At the same time he heard the distant rumble of jets and a crackling sound, so faint and irregular that at first he thought he might be imagining it.

The noise of the jets grew louder. Blade heard the crash and roar of sonic booms, and the metallic glints turned into a number of darting shapes. He saw a crimson glow leap across the sky, like a distant flash of weirdly-colored lightning. A little later he heard the crackling again.

Riyannah's eyes widened and she staggered to her feet, her numbness and exhaustion apparently gone in a moment. She stared at the sky as if by sheer willpower she could bring the distant machines closer.

They were moving steadily toward the two watchers on their own. The crimson flashes now came two or three times each minute. Blade saw smoke trails from jet exhausts and what looked like guided missiles. Several times he saw large grayish powder puffs of smoke, and once a huge black blossom with flame in its heart. Bits of debris trailed more smoke down from the explosion. He was seeing an aerial battle, but who was fighting?

Riyannah seemed to know, and she also seemed to care desperately. She stood as if turned to iron, eyes fixed on the battle, hands gripping her belt, face a frozen mask except for lips which moved silently, praying or cursing or doing something else outside Blade's understanding. He put a hand on her shoulder and spoke her name. He wanted to get both of them under cover before the battle got much closer and they were flattened by a stray missile.

It was no use. Trying to move Riyannah was like trying to move a statue. Before Blade could make up his mind to use brute force, the battle was almost on top of them. It took on a pattern, and then it was Blade's turn to freeze and stare at the sky.

He saw three different kinds of flying machines overhead. Two of them wore the red-bordered green triangle of the local government. One kind was the winged disks, the other was needle-nosed delta-wings, small and painted a glossy blue all over. Blade counted about half a dozen of each.

There were only two of the third kind. These were blunt-nosed arrow shapes, with a high tail fin but no wings, canopies, or engines Blade could make out. They were a dull gray all over, except for a black spot under the nose. As he watched, he saw the crimson glow dart out from the black spot, tracing a path through the air but dying out just short of one of the blue delta-wings. Some sort of energy weapon, obviously. Seen close up, it looked vaguely familiar. Blade had the distinct feeling he'd seen it somewhere, but he couldn't have said where to save his life.

It was also obvious that the two gray machines were losing the battle. They were badly outnumbered and one of them was already in trouble. It was slowly losing altitude, its sides were scarred and blackened from several hits, and smoke trailed from the base of its fin.

The other machine was flying a tight formation on its wounded comrade. From the way it whipped around in impossibly tight turns, Blade suspected the crew wasn't entirely human. Riyannah's people, no doubt. He was sure the second machine could have shown its tail to all the triangle-marked planes, and got safely away long ago. Instead it was staying to fight, almost certainly dooming itself as well.

It wasn't entirely a one-sided battle. The crimson beams weren't always accurate, but when they hit they were deadly. Blade saw a feeble flicker from the nose of the

30

damaged machine reaching out and taking one of the disks under its left wing. The wing curled up and tore loose, while the disk lurched, then spun wildly down to smash itself on the rocky hillside. The whole mouth of the valley vanished for a moment in a wall of smoke and flying wreckage, and Blade staggered as the concussion reached him.

That was the last victory of the gray machines. As its victim crashed, a pattern of four missiles bracketed the damaged one. Two hit, one blowing off the fin. The machine tipped up on its tail, pouring out blue smoke and white flame, then plunged vertically to the ground.

This time the explosion was so violent Blade wondered if it was atomic. The concussion knocked both him and Riyannah off their feet. Not only the valley but half the hills vanished behind the smoke, while chunks of metal and stone the size of a man's fist rattled down all around Blade.

The victors scattered in all directions, climbing, diving, making tight turns. One of the delta-wings turned a little too tightly. A wingtip grazed a hilltop and the machine flipped end over end, then vanished down the far side of the hill. Another pillar of smoke marked its end, but the half-deafened Blade never heard the explosion.

He was able to drag a weeping, unresisting Riyannah safely under the cover of the trees before the battle flared up again. The attackers circled at a safe distance from the mass of smoke. Twice disks passed so low overhead that Blade froze. He half-carried Riyannah the last few yards and laid her down on the softest patch of ground he could see, her rifle beside her. As he did, the second gray machine staggered out of the smoke.

It was still under control but it was rapidly losing altitude, belly and fin looking as if they'd been chewed by mice, and one side as black as if it had been painted. The machine fired a last feeble crimson beam, making a patch of rock on the hillside smoke. Then the beam generator seemed to explode, gushing yellowish smoke. Somehow the crew of the machine still kept it under control. Nose high, it floated down and struck the ground. It skidded for a quarter of a mile, lurching from side to side, trailing smoke and sparks. Then it slewed around and came to a stop barely two hundred yards from Blade.

31

Instantly two troop carriers popped over the hills and came whirring toward the fallen machine. The remaining jets formed a close umbrella over their victim as the troop carriers closed with it.

The fallen machine lay still and silent. Blade noticed that the smoke was diminishing, as the fire burned itself out or the crew got it under control. A hatch opened on the undamaged side of the machine, just ahead of the fin. Blade saw movement in the hatchway, and a moment later the first of the crew climbed out and dropped to the ground.

After so many trips to Dimension X, Blade was about as hard to surprise as a sane human very well could be. This Dimension had given him even more than its share of the unexpected. Yet he still found himself gaping as the crew of the gray machine climbed out.

There were four—*beings*—in the crew. They were nine feet tall, and resembled nothing so much as gigantic stalks of asparagus. Each had four double-jointed arms, ending in lobster-like claws. They swayed like trees in the wind as they moved.

They were called the Menel, they came from interstellar space and Blade had met them twice before. Both times they'd been enemies. Once he'd found them helping a scientist with a twisted mind create monsters called Ice Dragons, terrorizing and conquering. The other time they'd been trying for conquest on their own, using a Dimension's birds and animals as their weapons.

Both times Blade had tried his best to avoid killing the Menel except when absolutely necessary. He refused to slaughter intelligent aliens when there might be some hope of eventually communicating with them and establishing peaceful relations. He wasn't optimistic. The Menel seemed to be a race bent on conquest, skilled, efficient, brave, in some ways worthy of respect, but also thoroughly dangerous. If the humans of this Dimension were fighting the Menel, what should he do? He still couldn't like the soldiers, but it might not be a good idea to fight them. At least they wouldn't need his help, not if they could always do as well against the Menel as he'd seen them do today.

By now all four Menel were well clear of the crippled machine. Three of them had belts around their bodies just below the arms and various bags and boxes slung from the

32

belts. The fourth was obviously wounded. It staggered more than the others, there was a wide bandage on its head, and every so often one of its comrades would reach out a couple of arms to help it over a patch of rough ground. One Menel was carrying a heavy black tube, one of the portable projectors for the crimson ray. That was the only recognizable weapon in sight.

The four Menel came to a stop, halfway between Blade and the crashed machine. He considered moving Riyannah deeper into the trees, but was afraid of missing even a moment of the Menel's actions. He still knew far too little about them.

The long silence brought Riyannah back to awareness of the world around her. She sat up, shook her head, picked up her rifle, and started to get to her feet. Blade held a finger to his lips and motioned her to stay put. She shook her head, but stayed low as she came out to lie beside him, watching the Menel.

Then a great many things happened in what seemed like only a few seconds. The Menel carrying the black tube lifted it high with two arms, then smashed it down on the ground. All four Menel spread out, the three unwounded ones raising all their arms over their heads. It was as unmistakable a gesture of surrender as Blade had ever seen.

The two troop carriers landed and their hatches opened. A dozen soldiers climbed out of each one, rifles at the ready. Then all the soldiers aimed at the Menel and opened fire. From a turret on top of the second carrier, a heavy laser joined in.

The four Menel were not only dead before they hit the ground, they were almost torn to pieces. The blast of heavy bullets and laser beams smashed into them like some deadly machine. Bags of gear, chunks of flesh, whole arms flew into the air. A brief silence after the first burst, then the roar and crackling came again as bullets and lasers ravaged the fallen bodies.

Riyannah bounced to her feet as if on springs. She let out a madwoman's shriek, then raised her rifle and sighted in on the soldiers. Blade was just in time. Her finger was squeezing the trigger when he grabbed her by both ankles and jerked her feet out from under her. The rifle fired a short burst as she crashed to the ground, the noise fortunately lost in the heavier firing of the soldiers.

Blade tried to grab the rifle and found himself having to fight to keep Riyannah from sticking the bayonet into him. Her eyes were wide, her face was gray, and she babbled things which could not have been words in any sane language. She used all her strength, and there was more in her slender frame than Blade would have suspected. He could no longer hope to be gentle with her. He could only hope to get her under control before she did something to attract the attention of the soldiers and doom both of them.

Riyannah let go of the rifle and clawed at Blade's face, leaving deep scratches on both cheeks. He gripped her wrists, and she bit his right hand hard enough to draw blood. She opened her mouth and he clamped a hand over it, gripping one of her hands with the other and pinning her remaining arm under his body. He could feel all her muscles taut and quivering against him, and he began to wonder if he was going to have to knock her unconscious before she'd stop fighting. They had to get out of here fast! The soldiers might be searching the area before long.

Then the whole world turned glaring white as the light from an explosion swamped Blade's vision. The ground heaved under him, and a massive fist of shock-driven air picked up him and Riyannah and slammed them against a tree. For a moment Blade's world was black instead of white, and the roar in his head drowned out the roar of the explosion.

As Blade's hearing returned, he heard trees going over, branches falling, and chunks of metal pattering, clanging, and crashing down all around him. Something small hit him in the shoulder, searing through the cloth of his tunic into his skin. Something larger bounced off the helmet he'd wisely left on. Blade lay where he was, covering Riyannah with his body, until things stopped falling. She was sprawled on her back, unconscious but apparently unhurt. He shifted his weight off her without rising and looked toward the open ground.

He could barely see it. Where the Menel machine had been was a black crater pouring up smoke and surrounded by grotesquely twisted pieces of blackened metal. Some were larger than a man.

The four Menel were only scattered patches of ash, with a few recognizable bits here and there. The soldiers hadn't

34

been so lucky. They'd been alive when the blast struck them, and some of them still were, crawling blindly around and making animal noises. The two troop carriers lay on their sides, broken and burning. The smoke from them mixed with the smoke from the crater to lie like a sooty fog across the battlefield.

Blade got to his feet and started gathering his equipment. He was sure there was nothing more to be learned here, and he was even more sure he didn't want to stay around here any longer. Each act of violence he met in this Dimension seemed to be bigger and bloodier than the last one. Sooner or later he'd meet one big enough to swallow him up. A lone man had no place in a battle against the Menel, at least not when he didn't know any more than Blade did now.

He'd been lucky this time. Even so, every exposed inch of skin prickled as if he'd got a mild dose of poison ivy. Some sort of radiation from the explosion, no doubt. Well, the damage was done, and if he was going to drop down dead after a few steps there was no point in worrying about it beforehand. At least the explosion had wiped out the soldiers and thoroughly eliminated any danger of pursuit.

Blade finished adjusting straps and buttoning flaps. He slung Riyannah's rifle across his chest along with his own, then bent down and lifted her on his back. With all their weapons and gear plus her weight on his back, he felt like Atlas holding the world on his shoulders.

He managed to get into a regular stride, and in a few minutes they were deep inside the forest. He kept going, stubbornly putting one foot in front of another in spite of sweat pouring into his eyes and screams of protest from every muscle in his body, until he'd covered about two miles. Then he lowered Riyannah to the ground, caught his breath, went back, and brushed out the last hundred yards of his trail with a fallen branch. Finally he sat down, drank some water, and tried to make sense of what he'd just seen.

He didn't do very well. Obviously the Menel were trying to conquer this world, as they'd tried with the other two Dimensions where he met them. Just as obviously, the soldiers and airmen of this Dimension were putting up a stiff fight. They were being cruel, ruthless, and unpleasant about it, but they were fighting hard. Certainly they had reason to fight hard, and perhaps they had some reason to be ruthless, at least toward the Menel. What about Riyannah and her human friends?

Blade remembered Riyannah's hysterical rage at the sight of the Menel's defeat and death and her suicidal urge to avenge them by opening fire on the soldiers. That had to mean the Menel were friends, allies, perhaps soldiers of her people. In turn that meant her people were trying to conquer this Dimension, and her human allies were in fact traitors to their own people.

Blade found his thoughts taking an ugly turn. If Riyannah's people and the Menel were allies in an effort to conquer this Dimension, would he have to join the side of those brutal soldiers? Would he even be allowed to, or would they shoot him on sight? Should he turn Riyannah over to them after all, winning good treatment for himself and striking a blow against the Menel? Or should he just leave Riyannah somewhere and fade into the forest, saying "a plague on both your houses" to this whole damned Dimension?

It was a confusing situation, to say the least.

A man less tough-minded than Blade would have been paralyzed by the confusion. Even Blade had to sit longer than he'd intended before it became clear what he should do.

He would turn back the way he'd come, cross the mountains, and hide himself in the wilderness beyond them. The soldiers didn't seem to come there on foot, and he hadn't seen the Menel there at all. He'd be safe enough, at least for a while.

He would also take Riyannah with him. He would take her with him, if he had to tie her hand and foot and carry her every inch of the way! He had to keep her with him until he could learn her language or she could learn English. He wasn't sure how far he'd be willing to go if she was stubborn, but he suspected he'd be willing to go farther than usual with a woman.

He had to learn who she was and who were her people. He had to learn about everybody else involved in the war in this Dimension, the Menel above all. This was the first chance he'd ever had to find out exactly where the Menel came from. It might be his last.

It was no longer just a matter of satisfying his own curiosity, or even Lord Leighton's. It could be a matter of life or death—his own, and that of hundreds of millions of people in many different Dimensions.

Blade sighed. It seemed that the stakes got bigger every time he traveled into Dimension X.

Chapter 6

Riyannah was a dead weight on Blade's aching back as he tramped towards the south-east. He could only make a rough guess about directions, but he thought he could get them back to the river. Then it would be easy to follow it back upstream to the canyon.

As the woman remained unconscious, Blade began to worry. Could she have serious internal or head injuries which might not show on the surface? Or could she be pretending to be seriously hurt in order to get him off his guard? That would make sense if she now thought he was an enemy. Did she? Without being able to talk to her, it would be almost impossible for him to know until it was too late. Certainly she'd had her doubts about him, a man who killed her enemies but looked very much like them and spoke no language she could understand. She'd been willing to travel with him so far, but did she have any choice? Would she realize that he'd only prevented her from firing on the soldiers who'd killed the Menel to save her own life? A fine string of unanswerable questions!

Blade could be sure of only one thing. He'd have to learn to talk to Riyannah as quickly as possible, and in the meantime he'd watch her closely. He didn't want to make her so suspicious she turned into an enemy. He also didn't want to get a knife stuck into his ribs some night because Riyannah thought she was avenging her dead Menel comrades that way.

About twilight they reached a small stream. Blade lowered Riyannah to the ground, took a blanket out of the pack, and wrapped her in it. She woke up about the time Blade felt his muscles returning to normal. She lay there looking steadily at Blade. It was impossible to tell what she was feeling or thinking. The huge green eyes and the delicate features were totally without expression.

Her silvery hair was as tangled as a hedge, full of leaves and needles. Blade took a comb from his pack, washed it in the stream, sat down beside Riyannah, and gently began to comb out her hair. She flinched at the first touch of his hand, winced several times as he accidentally pulled her hair, but otherwise lay still. When he'd finished, she reached up, ran her fingers through her hair, then smiled faintly.

Blade smiled back, then picked up a canteen. *"Drink,"* he said, raising it to his lips and going through the motions of drinking. Then he poured a few drips on the ground. *"Water,"* he said.

Riyannah nodded and reached for the canteen. *"Water,"* she said, splashing some on her face. *"Drink,"* she said, and did so.

Blade would have continued the language lesson, but Riyannah soon drifted off to sleep again. Blade recognized the healthy sleep of a totally exhausted body. Carefully he gathered up the rifles, the knives, and everything else that might be used as a weapon. He strapped them all to his pack or put them inside it. Then he lay down, pulled a blanket over him, and pulled his pack under his head. The arrangement looked natural enough for Riyannah not to suspect anything, but she could hardly get at any of the weapons without waking Blade.

So far so good. Blade had the feeling he was going to be saying that to himself quite a few times before his trip through this Dimension was over. Then he stopped thinking about anything and fell asleep.

Blade returned to the wilderness beyond the canyon faster then he'd left it. Now he had clothes on his back, boots on his feet, and something beside raw fish and fruit in his belly. He also had a companion, but she didn't slow him down.

Once Riyannah slept off the shock and exhaustion of the fighting, she showed surprising strength. She couldn't carry as heavy a load as Blade, but she kept up with him every foot of the way. She would stagger the last few hundred yards of each day's march, but she always stayed on her feet to the end.

Riyannah also learned the English Blade taught her with surprising speed. She remembered practically everything, seldom had to be corrected, and even managed to pronounce most of the words correctly. By the end of the second day on the march, Blade had taught her nearly all the basic words they'd need for survival in the wilderness. The lack of communication between them was no longer so dangerous.

Blade didn't care to go farther than this with the language lessons, after one unsuccessful experiment. He drew pictures of various types of flying machines on the ground, then named them. Finally he drew a picture of the Menel machine and said:

"Spaceship."

He handed the stick to Riyannah and looked curiously at her. She looked back at him, meeting his eyes but not saying a word. Then she quickly scratched out the spaceship and turned her back on him, her shoulders quivering. She was silent for nearly half an hour.

She wasn't willing to trust him with any information about her own people or her own business. Blade wasn't surprised. She also probably realized that he didn't entirely trust her, so it was hardly fair to expect her to hand him all the information he needed on a silver platter!

Blade decided to let serious questions wait until they were a few days farther into the wilderness. Seeing that he wasn't going to behave like the soldiers might win her trust or at least get her off guard.

There was no point in even thinking about what intelligence services delicately called "physical methods"—torture. He was sure nothing he could do to her would make her say a word she didn't want to. He'd simply end up with a corpse, a bad conscience he'd carry to his grave, and no information to carry back to Home Dimension.

Getting back up through the canyon was a slower and wetter job than coming down through it. Several places where Blade had climbed down were completely impassable going the other way. By the time they came out at the wilderness end, it was nearly dark, a chill wind was blowing, and both of them were soaked to the skin up to their waists.

Blade decided to build a fire. The flying machines of either side might spot it, or it might attract the bat-cats. It was still worth the risk, when the alternative was spending the night shivering in wet clothes.

The soldiers carried something rather like a cigarette lighter, except that it generated a miniature laser beam instead of a flame. A handful of dry needles, leaves, and twigs caught the first time around. Blade piled on a few more chunks, then set a whole armload of wood on the ground beside the fire to dry out.

When the fire could be left to itself, Blade unpacked his gear, then pulled off his tunic and shirt. As he did, Riyannah frowned, then stared at him so intently Blade wondered if he'd sprouted a third arm. Then he realized what must be going through her mind. She thought his peeling off his clothes to dry them meant a sexual assault. She was getting ready to fight or run.

He laughed. "No, Riyannah, I do not—" then pointed to his groin, while shaking his head.

Riyannah's eyes shifted from his face to his groin, then back again. She seemed to relax slightly, but she was obviously still uncertain about something. Perhaps she wanted him out of sight so she could take off her own clothes.

Blade nodded. "Yes, Riyannah. I go—" pointing at a nearby tree, thick enough to hide three or four men.

This time Riyannah shook her head, clearly not just nervous but irritated. While Blade was still trying to figure out what the woman wanted now, she stood up and started unbuttoning her own shirt. Before Blade could say a word, she was bare to the waist. Her breasts were small firm cones, tipped with large dark nipples now hardening from desire or from the chill night air. The light of the fire played across her skin, covering it with a dappled, dancing pattern of shadows. Blade felt a familiar warmth in his groin, and his throat was tight. He'd seldom seen a more desirable woman.

He also hadn't been quite as confused about what to do with a desirable woman since he was fifteen. He'd have sworn that sex was the last thing on Riyannah's mind. She'd been raped, she must be exhausted, and in any case she didn't trust him. Yet here she was, calmly peeling off her clothes.

By now Riyannah had her boots off. She stood up, unbuckled her trousers, shoved them down her legs, and stepped out of the pile. With the light and shadows now playing over the rest of her body, she was even more exquisite. Blade found the warmth in his groin turning into a fire.

He started taking off the rest of his own clothes, since she clearly wanted him to do that much. After that he'd let her take the lead and see what happened. If it came to sex, he'd make sure they lay down someplace away from the weapons.

By the time Blade was naked, Riyannah was covered from head to toe with gooseflesh. She stared at Blade's penis as if she'd never seen anything like it before, or as if there was something unusual about it. Neither explanation really made sense. Riyannah was hardly an innocent girl, and there was nothing unusual about Blade's penis. It was now impressively erect, but that was only to be expected in the presence of a desirable, naked, and apparently willing woman.

Riyannah went on staring at Blade's penis, occasionally meeting his eyes but always looking down again afterward. Blade began to feel gooseflesh on his own skin, at least on the side away from the fire.

Riyannah finally stopped looking at Blade's erection, then licked her lips and stepped forward. She came around the fire and knelt in front of Blade. Then she gently laid three fingers on his penis and pushed it to one side. Her head was now within inches of Blade's groin.

Was she going to use her mouth on him? That would be a pleasant surprise. Those long slim fingers were moving on his penis with great gentleness and maddening skill. If her lips had some of that same skill, he could hope for—

Riyannah's fingers stopped their movement. Still holding Blade's penis, she sat back on her heels. Again her eyes traced a path up and down his body. Blade thought he detected surprise and confusion on her face this time. Apparently she'd found something she hadn't expected, or not found something she'd been expecting.

Blade stopped feeling pleased and excited over the prospect of sex with Riyannah and began to feel annoyed. He was getting a little tired of being stared at as if he was something rare and monstrous. If there was something unusual about him, he'd be damned if he knew what it was!

He reached down and gently plucked Riyannah's fingers from his penis. She looked up at him and smiled. He thought she was fighting not to laugh. Then she bent swiftly, planted a kiss on Blade's penis, stood up, backed away to the other side of the fire, and started pulling on her clothes.

She didn't even look at Blade until she was fully dressed. Then she piled some more wood on the fire and smiled at him again. It was a slow, gentle smile that seemed to spread all across her face. Normally her face was rather austere, everything except the eyes small, the flesh stretched too tightly over the bones. The smile transformed it, giving warmth, substance, even sensuousness. If Riyannah hadn't just refused an opportunity for sex, Blade would have been quite sure he was getting an explicit invitation.

Riyannah seemed to feel he was a mystery, perhaps a dangerous one for her people and the Menel. So she was playing a game of her own, trying to solve the mystery of Richard Blade the same way he was trying to solve the mystery of Riyannah. That could make things harder for him in one way, Blade realized. Riyannah would now have her guard up and be watching him closely. On the other hand, there was also one advantage.

If he was a mystery she needed to solve, she'd also need to keep him alive for a while. Blade suspected he shouldn't have to worry any more about her sticking a knife into him some night. Now he could spend more time watching for the dangers of the wilderness instead of watching his own back.

That was just as well. They'd both live a lot longer that way.

Chapter 7

Riyannah might be alert and watching him, but that didn't keep Blade from trying to find out who she was and where she came from. He tried three more times in the next few days as they marched deeper into the wilderness.

Once he tried drawing spaceships again. A second time he started a conversation on the stars in the night sky. A third time he tried to make a joke about her examination of his penis, wondering out loud what was wrong with it? She laughed and that lovely sensuous smile spread across her face again, but she didn't answer the question.

Once they'd passed through the canyon, they turned north away from the river and the cliffs along its south bank. The river was too easy a mark for anyone searching for them, and the cliffs seemed to shelter too many of the bat-cats. The country was so lush and green there had to be plenty of water and game everywhere.

If they got far enough from the river, it might also keep Riyannah from trying to run away. For all her courage, strength, and endurance, she seemed to be something of a babe in the woods when it came to wilderness survival. Apart from everything else, if she tried to run off, she would probably get lost. Then she might very well die before Blade could find her, if he could find her at all.

Blade didn't want that. She might be an enemy, or at least the friend and ally of the Menel, who certainly were enemies. He still didn't like to think of her fleeing into the forest, to die of exposure or starvation or being torn apart by wild animals. He was getting used to waking each morning and seeing her asleep in her blankets on the other side of the campfire. Asleep, her small face had an innocence that made it almost possible to believe she really was a child.

Four days march north of the river, Blade set up a permanent camp. The cliffs along the river were far out of sight to the south. The mountains to the north were looming higher and higher. Blade could see the blue-white shimmer of the glaciers along their flanks and feel a new chill in the air. The country was well-watered, with a spring or clear stream every mile or so. It had plenty of birds, small animals, and edible berries, and apparently no bat-cats. Finally, Blade hadn't seen or heard any sort of plane in two days. He and Riyannah might have been Adam and Eve, alone in a newly-created world.

The only serpent in their Eden was that each of them still had to learn the other's secrets without revealing their own.

For the first few days at the camp, Blade was too busy getting them settled in to worry about Riyannah's secrets. There was shelter to build, firewood to gather, snares to set for animals, and a water supply to establish. Blade could work beside Riyannah for hours on end without remembering that she was a mystery he had to solve.

If Blade suspected before that Riyannah didn't know much about living in the wilderness, he was now absolutely sure. She learned quickly what he taught her, but he had to teach her practically everything. She watched him building their shelter as if he'd been conjuring a palace out of the ground by waving a magic wand.

Within three days they were as comfortable and safe as they could hope to be. They had shelter, food, water, and weapons. The branches overhead grew so thickly that the shelter and even the fire were invisible from no more than a hundred feet up.

Their days settled into a peaceful routine. Every morning they washed in a nearby stream. Riyannah now stripped in Blade's presence as casually as if they'd been lovers for years. She never came close to him while they were bathing, though. Blade was quite willing to leave things that way.

After bathing, they ate a breakfast of leftovers from last night's dinner. Then while Riyannah tidied things up, Blade would go check his snares and the lines he'd left in a stream a mile to the west. He relied on them for most of the food. They had two hundred rounds of rifle ammunition and five grenades, but Blade wanted them saved for future emergencies. He doubted they'd have any serious trouble in the forest. They seemed to be outside the hunting grounds of the bat-cats and he hadn't seen anything else large enough to be dangerous. Leaving the woods might be another matter when it came to fighting.

Without those thoughts of the future, Blade might have been tempted to pitch the rifles, ammunition, and grenades into the nearest stream. It was getting harder to stay on his guard and keep all the weapons out of Riyannah's hands. At the same time she never made a single move toward any of them. Did this mean she could really be trusted, or was she playing an even deeper game than he suspected? Blade would have given a great deal to know—and even more not to have to ask the question at all.

Damn it, Riyannah was too pleasant a companion to be caught up in this "war of the worlds," Menel or no Menel. To be sure, some of the most pleasant companions could also be deadly opponents. Blade learned that very young, and because of that lived to grow older. He didn't have to like it.

Blade always spent most of the morning collecting the night's catch and resetting the snares and lines. They spent the afternoon working around the camp, collecting wood, mushrooms, and berries, and cooking dinner. All this kept them so busy they seldom had to talk about anything except the "safe" topics—food, the weather, Blade's luck with the fish, the bugs in the bedding. Riyannah knew all the English she needed for this sort of talk. Sometimes the conversation flowed on pleasantly for half an hour, until suddenly one or the other realized they were drifting over toward dangerous ground.

They ate dinner as the forest darkened, then banked up the fire. By the time it was dark, they were both rolled up in their blankets, sound asleep on the opposite sides of the shelter. Each night the last thing Blade heard was Riyannah's gentle breathing. He was getting used to hearing it.

In the darkness of the seventh night at the camp, Blade awoke. Something was crying out in the forest, far off and distorted by distance but still loud enough to wake him. He sat up, throwing off the blankets with one hand and gripping his rifle with the other as he listened for the cries to come again.

They did. He heard a high-pitched screaming, something

which might have been a growl, then a deep-toned bellowing. Another growl, fading away, then silence except for the wind and the call of a night bird.

Blade looked at Riyannah. She'd turned over, but her eyes were still closed and her breathing as slow and regular as ever. Even if she'd heard anything, she wasn't likely to remember it next morning.

The fire was down to a pile of dimly-glowing coals puffing up smoke. Chill air crept into the shelter and flowed across Blade's skin, biting in a way he hadn't felt before. The thought of going back to sleep was enormously appealing.

Instead he forced himself to stay awake for another hour, listening for more cries in the night. He only heard more night birds and the sigh of the wind, Riyannah's breathing, and the occasional *pop* of a live coal. At last he tossed another handful of sticks on the fire, wrapped himself up in his blankets, and slept peacefully until Riyannah shook him awake in a clear, cool dawn.

Blade spent the morning collecting the night's catch: four fish and something like a cross between a gopher and a duck-billed platypus. He spent the afternoon exploring the area around the camp almost tree by tree, looking for signs of whatever made the cries in the night.

Just before dinnertime he found what he was looking for. In the middle of a patch of churned-up earth, half buried in dead leaves and needles, sprawled a large animal. It reminded Blade of a short-legged moose with a shaggy coat and a long curling tail. Two pairs of broad antlers jutted out from either side of the narrow skull, bending upward at right angles. The animal looked as if it was wearing a pair of bookends on its head.

The animal was so badly mangled that Blade could hardly tell where one injury ended and another began. The neck was broken, the skull cracked and the brains eaten out, the belly slashed open and most of the internal organs gone, and the rump eaten down to the bone. The killers had been hungry as well as powerful.

Searching the area around the body, Blade turned up two kinds of footprints. One was broad and round, obviously the dead animal's. The other showed six long toes spreading out like a fan, each tipped with a claw. Blade counted at least three different sets of the second kind.

So much for his notion that this part of the forest was clear of dangerous animals. He looked around him carefully, estimating the size of the clearing. He wished now that he'd seen more of the bat-cats in action when he was in the wilderness the first time. Could they climb trees and glide across clearings, or could they attack entirely on the ground?

Blade snapped off the safety on his rifle and worked a round into the chamber. Then he headed back to camp, following a deliberately confused route, frequently stopping to listen, and trying to look in all directions at once. He heard and saw nothing, but suddenly the forest no longer seemed so friendly.

What next? Moving the camp farther north would take a lot of time and hard work, and might be wasted effort. If the bat-cats laired in the cliffs along the river, they might also nest along the slopes of the mountains to the north. Going north could be jumping out of the frying pan into the fire.

On the other hand, staying where they were meant arming Riyannah. She had to be able to defend herself against the bat-cats, and there was only one way to be sure of that. Forcing her to stay in camp wouldn't work even if she was willing. A pack of the big cats could rip the shelter apart and get at anyone inside it. So she'd have to take one of the rifles and a magazine of ammunition. That should be enough for dealing with the bat-cats.

It would also be more than enough to let her shoot him in the back if she felt like it. He had to take the chance. If the bat-cats killed Riyannah, her secrets would die with her. Blade didn't like the prospect any more than he liked the thought of being shot in the back.

In fact, he didn't like the thought of Riyannah dying at all. He had a duty to keep her alive, at least until something happened to make it an equally clear duty to kill her. It wasn't just a duty to Home Dimension, either. It was a duty to his own conscience. Blade knew he wasn't in love with Riyannah. He also knew that if he killed her or let her die through a mistake of his, he'd find it very hard to forget her or forgive himself.

Richard Blade, he thought. *You are going to have to ask yourself whether you are getting too soft for this kind of work.* Then he shrugged and put the question out of his mind. Whatever answer he got when he was safely back in Home Dimension, it would make no difference here and now.

Blade nearly ran the last few hundred yards to the camp. Riyannah was walking off toward the nearest spring to refill their canteens.

"Riyannah!" he shouted, waving furiously. She turned. "Come here!" As she hurried toward him, he pulled a magazine out of his pack and picked up her empty rifle. Then he shoved the magazine into place, snapped on the safety, pulled out the bayonet, and locked it on to the rifle's muzzle. By now Riyannah was back in the camp, looking curiously at him. Before she could say anything, he held the rifle out to her.

"Here, Riyannah. Take this. It is yours."

Riyannah stared at it as if he'd slapped her, grabbed for the rifle, and missed. It fell to the ground with a thud. She knelt to pick it up, but her hands were shaking so badly she couldn't grip it. Her eyes shut, squeezing out tears which washed paths through the soot on her face.

"Why?" she said, in a voice so strangled that Blade could barely understand her.

"There are dangerous animals in this forest. I did not think there were any, but now I know I was wrong. You must have a rifle and ammunition, to defend yourself against the animals."

"You did—I—", then a wordless choking noise. For a moment Riyannah seemed too stunned and confused even to cry, let alone speak.

"I do not want you to be killed by the animals," said Blade, smiling. "Why should I? That would make me stupid and cruel, like the soldiers."

Slowly, as if all her joints were rusty, Riyannah stood up. Her fists were clenched and her eyes were open but staring blindly. Then she stepped forward, tripped over the rifle, and nearly fell into Blade's arms.

He held her gently and kissed her on the forehead and on the eyes until she stopped shaking. At last she straightened up and he let her go. She stepped back and nearly tripped over the rifle.

Blade laughed. "Riyannah, the first thing you must learn about this rifle is not to jump up and down on it." She laughed in turn, bent down, and picked it up.

49

"You will teach me how to shoot the animals?" she said. "I know this gun, but only—" She fumbled for the words, then went through a pantomime of firing it from the hip on full automatic. "Is that good for the animals too?"

"No. With the animals, you must fire one shot at a time. But I will teach you that, and other things as well. Then you will be safe from the animals as long as we are in the forest." This was the first time he'd even hinted they might sooner or later be moving on.

"What if there are more animals than there are shots for the rifles?"

"Then—" He hesitated, then decided to take the risk. "Then I suppose we will have to go somewhere else, where there are no dangerous animals. Do you know such a place?"

Only a trained eye like Blade's could have detected Riyannah's little gasp and the slight stiffening of the slender body. She licked her lips three times, one fist still clenched. For a moment Blade could have sworn she was going to answer, "Yes," and perhaps say even more.

Then the moment passed. She frowned and slowly shook her head. "I do not think I know such a place. Do you?"

"No."

"Then we must make this place safe for both of us. Is that not true, Blade?"

This time he reached out and drew her to him with one arm, to kiss her on both cheeks. She did not protest, but smiled up at him until he let her go.

Chapter 8

Blade and Riyannah went out into the woods for a little target practice. Blade fired five rounds at a tree fifty yards away to show Riyannah how to aim. Then he watched as she fired ten rounds herself. On the eleventh round the tree fell over, cut completely through.

Blade decided that was enough practice. Riyannah wasn't going to be another Annie Oakley, but she could aim the rifle and didn't freeze on the trigger. Blade knew trained soldiers who couldn't hit the broad side of a barn unless they were standing inside it or firing on full automatic. Riyannah could certainly put at least one bullet into anything the size of a bat-cat before it could get to her. With the heavy slugs the rifles fired, one should be enough to stop a bat-cat or anything else smaller then an elephant.

Blade also told Riyannah, "Do not go out of the camp alone if I am close enough to be called. If you must go out alone, always take your rifle. Leave the safety on, but keep looking upward and be ready to fire if you see anything suspicious."

Blade still didn't know if the bat-cats would be a menace or only a nuisance. He thought of strengthening the shelter, then decided against it. Before he could build anything able to resist the bat-cats, he and Riyannah would probably be on the move again.

Giving Riyannah her own rifle and ammunition made it very clear he trusted her. That display of trust had wiped out much of her suspicion of him. She'd already been on the edge of revealing something important. Next time she might go ahead and reveal it, and then what? Blade didn't know, but he suspected it would mean leaving the wilderness.

51

The prospect of facing bat-cats didn't change their daily routine much. Blade built bigger fires at night and made his morning trips shorter. When they bathed, they bathed one at a time, the other sitting on the bank with rifle in hand and eyes on the sky.

The trees around their bathing place grew thinly, leaving more open sky than Blade liked. On the other hand, the next nearest place for bathing was two miles away, and the path to it led through several large clearings. Unless bat-cats could land on a dime, they were safer where they were.

Certainly the beasts were prowling the forest. Three nights in a row Blade awoke to their screams and growls. They were never as close as they'd been the first night, and he never bothered looking for their victims. He wondered what was bringing them into this part of the forest all at once. The nights seemed to be growing colder. Was the change in the weather causing a migration of the wildlife, so that the bat-cats had to follow their food supply? If so, how thickly would they gather? Too many carnivores in any one area would eat the forest bare of game. Unfortunately it wouldn't take too many bat-cats to make the area of the camp unpleasant for Blade and Riyannah.

On the tenth night, the screams of the bat-cats and the wild cries of their victims were louder than ever before. Either they were hunting closer to the camp or it was a larger pack. Blade not only woke up but found it uncomfortably hard to get back to sleep. He finally dozed off again as the forest outside began to turn gray.

He awoke to find Riyannah curled up snugly against him, her own blankets lying rumpled and discarded in her corner of the shelter. She was naked, and for such a slim woman she gave off a surprising amount of warmth.

Blade took Riyannah gently by the shoulders and kissed her even more gently. He had to fight to keep his lips and hands from moving on down her body, or even to pull them away. As he crept out from under the blankets, she turned over with a gentle sigh, blinked, then went back to sleep.

She didn't wake up until Blade was fully dressed. Then she rolled out from under the blankets, pulled on her own clothes, and smiled at Blade. As usual, the smile turned her face into something warm and appealing. It also hinted that she'd known exactly what she was doing when she crawled under his blankets.

Half an hour later, Riyannah was naked again. She climbed out of the stream, raising both hands to wring out her hair. The motion lifted her breasts and formed the rest of her slim body into a graceful curve, like a bent bow. Her nipples were hard and dark in the chill of the morning and beads of water stood out on her skin.

Her skin was a shade darker than before, from weeks of soot and grease no cold-water scrubbing could remove. It hadn't lost any of its beauty, though. Her silver-white pubic triangle stood out like a beacon. The sunlight shining through the trees overhead turned the drops of water on her skin into sparkling jewels and threw moving patterns of light and shade on her throat, shoulders, and breasts. Riyannah might not be at home in the wilderness, but she certainly looked enough like a wild creature of the forest and the waters.

At last Riyannah stopped posing, got dressed, and sat down on a boulder with her rifle across her knees. Blade's rifle rested muzzle up against the boulder. Blade stripped off his clothes, except for the knife in a sheath on his right ankle, and plunged into the stream.

The biting chill took his breath away, as it always did at first. He went deep, letting the current carry him downstream, then swept upward toward the sunlight and the air.

As his head broke surface, Riyannah screamed. Blade shot half clear of the water like a leaping dolphin, then turned toward Riyannah.

Three bat-cats were gliding out of the sky at her. Their tails were rigid, their membranes fully spread, their forepaws reaching out, and their eyes fixed hungrily. Blade was twenty yards downstream from Riyannah and nearly on the opposite bank. The bat-cats were too intent on Riyannah to care about any other prey. He ducked under and churned toward the woman.

Her rifle went off, the sound distorted by the water, a bat-cat screamed, and the rifle fired three more times. Blade surfaced, and a bat-cat plunged into the stream almost on top of him. He drew his knife, then saw that half the beast's head was blown away by Riyannah's bullets.

Then the rifle jammed. As the second bat-cat came at

her, Riyannah thrust at it with the bayonet. The bat-cat saw what was waiting for it, tried to twist aside in midair, and failed. A hundred and fifty pounds of fur and claws, bone and sinew impaled itself on Riyannah's bayonet. The bat-cat screamed and spat and hissed more like a snake than an animal. It thrashed frantically, foam on its lips. Riyannah screamed as the dying bat-cat's writhing tore the rifle out of her hands. Then she screamed again as it rolled into the stream, taking the rifle with it.

Riyannah spent one second too long screaming. She lunged toward Blade's rifle leaning against the rock. The third bat-cat landed right on top of the rock, knocking the rifle to the ground. Riyannah jumped back as sharp claws flailed at her, slashing her trousers without breaking the skin underneath. She sprang backward, tripped over a root, and went down. The bat-cat's growl drowned out Riyannah's next scream. The beast let out a hiss and gathered itself to spring.

Then three more bat-cats sailed down out of the sky, landing beyond the boulder. The first bat-cat checked the spring which could have torn Riyannah to shreds in the next second. Before anything else could happen, Blade leaped out of the water with a yell.

He put all his lungpower into that yell, and it paralyzed all four bat-cats for a moment. Blade swung up onto the bank, pivoted on one foot, and smashed the other into the side of the first bat-cat. One of Blade's back kicks could crack a brick wall. The bat-cat flew off the top of the boulder, smashed into a tree ten feet away, and fell to the ground as limp as an empty balloon.

Blade dove for the rifle, but another bat-cat launched its spring first. Blade swerved and ducked in the same movement, so that the bat-cat's spring brought it down inches from his left foot. He leaped high and came down with both feet on the beast's neck before it could realize what was happening. Then he jumped to the ground, picked up the dead body by the tail, and hurled it into the faces of the other two bat-cats. They backed away, snarling and hissing defiantly. Then they dug in their hind feet and got ready to leap at Blade together.

A moment's hesitation had nearly been fatal to Riyannah. Now it was fatal to the bat-cats. Blade snatched up the rifle, snapped off the safety, and switched the selector to automatic. He squeezed the trigger as the bat-cats soared into the air, and the burst raked them from heads to bellies. They seemed to bounce backward as if they'd struck a wall of rubber, then collapsed on the ground. One of them writhed briefly, but that ended when Blade jabbed a bayonet into the base of its skull. Then there was silence in the forest except for the faint *plok-plok-plok* of water dripping off Blade.

Blade snapped on the safety and turned to Riyannah. She'd managed to struggle to her feet, but her face was still a pale coffee color under the dirt. He held the rifle out to her.

"Take this and watch for more bat-cats. I'm going to dive into the stream and try to get the other rifle back."

"Blade, do you think we need it so badly that you should put yourself in danger again?"

"I don't think there's any real danger. If more bat-cats come, try to get up into a tree before you start shooting. I imagine they can climb trees, but they'll be better targets for you while they're climbing."

Riyannah nodded and her hands steadied as they closed on the rifle. Blade turned away and plunged into the stream again.

He could only guess where the rifle might be and what could have happened to it, but luck was with him. The rifle not only stayed in the bat-cat's body, it weighted the body down enough to make it sink quietly to the bottom of the stream. On his third dive Blade saw the rifle sticking up like a flagpole. On the fourth dive he got his hands on it, and on the fifth he jerked it free. He came to the surface, gulped in air, then scrambled out onto the bank and began drying himself.

Riyannah didn't seem to be hurt at all, but she walked slowly on the way back to camp. Blade let her set the pace, though his feet itched to break into a run and his fingers itched to strip and oil the salvaged rifle. It was half their arsenal, and he was quite sure they hadn't seen the last of the bat-cats.

They reached camp without seeing or hearing any more of the beasts. Blade quickly built the fire up to a roaring blaze, spread a blanket on the ground beside it, then started laying out the parts of the rifle.

"Riyannah, there's a can of oil in your pack. Get it out,

will you?" Blade spoke without raising his eyes from his work. When silence followed his words, he looked up. She was nowhere in sight.

"Riyannah?" He started to get up. Then she stepped out of the shelter, wrapped from shoulders to knees in her blanket.

"Riyannah, did you get the—?"

He broke off as she shrugged her shoulders and let the blanket slip to the ground. Then she stepped toward him, naked and laughing, with a glow in her eyes that seemed to flow down and light up her skin as well. Slowly Blade put the rifle bolt down on the blanket. Then he rose to his feet and opened his arms to Riyannah.

She came up to him, then laughed and pressed both palms against his chest. "Blade, your clothes!"

"You're right." He knelt and began unlacing his boots. As he did, he was very much aware of Riyannah's soft breath on his cheek and in his ear, and her breasts almost in his face as she bent over him.

Blade finished with his boots and stood up. Riyannah knelt, unbuckled his belt with one hand, and unzipped his trousers with the other hand. This time when Riyannah's lips drifted down onto his flesh, they stayed there.

They stayed there until the warmth in Blade's groin became heat, then a form of delicious agony he couldn't have described to save his life. Half his mind and body wanted those lips to continue their work until the agony came to an end in fierce release. The other half of his mind and body wanted her to leave him for a moment while he stripped off the rest of his clothes.

Riyannah got the message. Her hands met his at the waist of his trousers, and all four hands together pushed Blade's pants down his legs. He stripped off his shirt and flung it high and far, careless of where it might land. Riyannah pressed herself hard against him and he felt the warm dampness between her legs and the firm points of her nipples. She groaned, and something seemed to stop Blade's breath in his throat. His head was swimming and the world spun around him as he lifted Riyannah in his arms and carried her into the shelter.

The blankets were outside and the needles and leaves on the floor dry and stiff. Neither of them cared. Blade sat down. Riyannah put both hands against his chest and pushed. He let her push him over, then reached up and cupped her breasts with his hands. She moaned as his fingers played with her nipples. Then she was straddling him and lowering herself onto him.

Her cry held both pain and pleasure as he entered her. Then she was swaying back and forth, with small movements which grew quickly wilder. Her hair whipped about her shoulders like windblown leaves, her face tightened bit by bit into a mask, and once again Blade felt agony and delirious pleasure at the same time. Now it only started in his groin, then spread swiftly through his whole body. He could not think, he could not see or hear, he could barely breathe. Riyannah was drawing all his senses into her, as she'd already drawn his swollen flesh.

Then Riyannah's body arched backward, until her hair flowed down to brush Blade's ankles and her eyes stared blankly up at the ceiling of the hut. She jerked convulsively once, twice, three times, mouth open but not a sound coming out. Waves of color came and went across her skin and tears flowed down her cheeks. Then Blade stopped noticing what was happening to Riyannah. His breath went out of him in a thick, choking cry as the agony went out of him in a series of fierce hot spurtings. He drove his hips upward as Riyannah clamped her thighs about him, and they heaved and tossed and thrashed about.

The magnificent moments passed. Blade heard his breathing and Riyannah's, felt the needles and leaves sandpapering his bare skin, smelled the cool mustiness of the shelter and the sharper odor of burning cloth—

Blade started and slapped Riyannah on the buttocks. "Let me up—quick!" He sprang to his feet so violently his head crashed into the roof of the shelter, bringing down a shower of twigs and needles. Then he dashed out into the open.

The blanket where he'd laid the parts of the rifle was sending up a haze of gray-brown smoke. As he watched, one edge began to turn black and little flames danced up. Blade clutched the other edge and yanked hard. Several parts rolled off into the dirt. Blade snatched up a log of firewood and hammered at the burning edge of the blanket as if he was pounding the life out of a deadly enemy.

At last the fire was out. Blade gathered up the scattered

parts, blew the dirt off them, and was putting them back on the blanket when he heard Riyannah laughing.

"Blade, are you—is this a thing your people do after sex? Pounding on the ground with a piece of wood?" Her laugh became a giggle.

Blade shook his head. "No. My people do many odd things, but this not not one of them."

"Will you tell me more about your people, if I tell you about mine? I do not know who or what your people are, but they must be quite interesting."

Now Blade felt like jumping up and down or running around the camp several times, shouting at the top of his lungs. The door to Riyannah's secrets was opening at last, opened by trust, shared danger, and shared passion.

"I do not know if you will call my people interesting or not. I will tell you about them, though."

"Good. But you can do that after you come to me again. Unless—you cannot—?"

"No, Riyannah, I am not old and feeble yet." The mere thought of having her in his arms again, was enough to revive him.

"Very good. Then come back to me. This shelter is warmer when there are two in it."

"True." He was barely inside before Riyannah's slim arms locked themselves around his waist.

Chapter 9

They made love three more times that day. They would have made love a fourth time, except that Riyannah finally admitted her left ankle was hurting her. Blade carefully examined it and decided she'd only pulled a couple of muscles. He laid cold cloths on it to reduce the swelling, then bound it tightly in strips of bark.

"Stay off it for a couple of days and you'll be able to walk again without any trouble. That's good, because I have a feeling we may have to move out of here before long."

"The bat-cats?"

"Yes. They aren't the most pleasant neighbors."

"Where do you think we should go? Do you have—a *spaceship* of your own?"

Blade was pleasantly tired after so much lovemaking, but his mental reflexes were still fast. He could recognize a leading question when he heard one.

"Not any more. What about you?"

"I hope I still do. If I do, it will be in the mountains to the north. I was going to take you to it. Then we saw the battle between the Targans and the Menel." She was silent for a moment, shutting her eyes as if trying to shut out the memory of the battle. Then she went on.

"You did come to Targa in a spaceship, I suppose?"

Blade smiled. "What else? Do you think I walked?"

Riyannah laughed. "No. Not that. But your people seem to have so many gifts, and they look so much like the Targans—"

"Riyannah," Blace said. "Once you complained I was trying to teach you too many new words too quickly. Now I say the same to you. What is Targa? Who are the Menel? Where will we go in your spaceship when we find it?" He stroked her hair. "Riyannah, you say I am from a

59

people with many gifts. This may be so. But I don't have the gift of being able to see what is in your mind and understand everything you say, whether you explain it or not. I think it is time you did what you promised—tell me about your world, and what you are doing here. Then I will tell you about my world and my people."

Riyannah smiled and kissed him. "That is only fair."

That was the last time either of them smiled or laughed for a couple of days. For Riyannah, it was too much of a strain, learning hundreds of new words in English while she told of the crisis facing her people and their allies the Menel.

For Blade, what he was hearing was simply too awesome to leave him feeling like laughing.

Riyannah came from a planet called Kanan, revolving around a yellow star very much like Blade's own sun. After a little comparing of units of measurement, Blade knew that Kanan's star must be at least thirty light-years away from wherever he was now.

"I will show you Ba-Kanan—the Father of Kanan—when we reach my spaceship. The telescope is powerful enough."

The Kananites also had faster-than-light travel. Riyannah came to this planet Targa in a spaceship which crossed the thirty light-years in three weeks. She'd planned to be back home on Kanan in less than a year of that planet's time.

As Riyannah described it, Kanan sounded like a paradise based on a technology centuries beyond Home Dimension's wildest dreams. The Kananites could generate, control, transmit, and store almost any amount of energy more or less at will. They derived most of what they needed at home from the sun, since it was the cheapest. Their crimson-beamed hurd-ray projectors could burn through armor plate, but their power came from storage cells no larger than a flashlight battery.

"We use guns firing solid shot only when we go into the wilderness," said Riyannah. "They are not so powerful as the Targan rifles." She paused. "Richard—forgive me if this is a question you cannot answer. But—you seemed very familiar with guns like the Targans'. Do your people use the same sort of weapon?"

Blade nodded. "We have found them good enough, as long as we do not go far from the ammunition supply."

"Ah, that explains it. We travel so far among the stars that we would have to take a whole factory with us if we or the Menel used weapons like yours."

Blade nodded again. "Yes. We do not yet travel among the stars as much as you or the Menel." That was perfectly true, as far as it went. "Now I have a question for you. You speak of going into the wilderness on Kanan. Yet you act like someone who has never been in wild country in her life. You're strong and brave and you learn quickly. But I had to teach you much you should already have known if you'd really spent much time in a true wilderness. What *do* you have on Kanan?"

Riyannah looked at the ground for a moment and Blade saw the slow darkening of her cheeks which was her blush. Then she said. "I suppose there is no reason not to tell you the truth. It will perhaps make you think badly of the Kananites, but there is no help for that."

"If the Kananites can travel among the stars and are all as brave as you are, I will never think badly of them," said Blade. "So what is the awful truth about Kanan?"

The Kananites made most of their discoveries about energy more than a thousand years before. Since that time they'd abolished war and poverty, controlled their population, and shaped their whole planet to suit their tastes.

The one billion Kananites lived in twenty gigantic cities of mile-high towers, enjoying every possible luxury. Around the cities were the spaceports and the factories which made everything the Kananites needed, including their food.

The rest of the planet was nearly uninhabited. Part of it was real wilderness, like the land where Blade and Riyannah were now. The wild animals roamed there, the glaciers crunched down the mountainsides, the snow fell and the flowers bloomed as if there wasn't a single intelligent being on the planet.

The Kananites never went into the true wilderness. They hiked and swam and hunted in areas closer to the cities, equipped with shelters, free of wild animals—in short a "tame" wilderness. Few Kananites ever spent a night in the open, picked berries for food, or built their own shelters. Their "wilderness" was fine for getting

61

healthy exercise, fresh air, and sunshine, but not for learning to survive outdoors.

The Kananites were not decadent. They understood both the pleasure and the need for the outdoor life. At the same time they weren't willing to give up the comforts they'd known all their long lives.

Kananite medicine was as advanced as the rest of their science. Riyannah was over a hundred Home Dimension years old and she could expect to live to nearly three hundred. That made Blade think even more highly of her courage. She'd been willing to give up two hundred years of life for whatever cause brought her here. It also made him realize why most Kananites were so cautious and conservative. How had they managed to build an empire among the stars in spite of this?

"An empire?" said Riyannah when Blade raised the question. "You mean—many planets settled by Kananites?"

"Something like that, yes."

She laughed. "Why should we want to do that when we have everything we could hope to need at home? Besides, some of the other planets might someday have their own people. So we should leave those planets alone." Her face hardened. "The Targans think differently. They would take Kanan itself if they could."

The Kananites traveled, explored, studied the geology and wildlife of the planets they discovered, but seldom stayed for more than a few years. When a planet was settled for longer than that, it was usually the Menel who settled it.

The asparagus-shaped Menel were the only other advanced race the Kananites had discovered in their star-traveling. Although the Menel were more warlike than the Kananites, it turned out to be possible to win their friendship and support.

"We gave them some of our solar-energy converters and power cells," Riyannah said. "They quickly learned how to make more themselves. After that they would not fight us, we gave them the hurd-ray projectors and other weapons."

That was more than five hundred years ago. Since then the Menel worked with the Kananites as scouts, explorers, and sometimes guards or soldiers. The Kananites hadn't met any other space-traveling races, but they'd met several primitive ones. Not all of these were friendly, and sometimes the hurd-ray in the claws of the Menel had to be turned loose.

The Menel were ingenious, handy with machinery, physically rugged, brave, and loyal to both their own people and the Kananites. "We have never had a serious fight with them," said Riyannah. "Sometimes a Menel leader will go mad and try to make his followers turn against the Kananites. But other Menel will always stop him before much harm is done. They know that a war between our two peoples would cripple or destroy both. And you know how bravely they fight."

"Yes. The Menel in the two ships were very brave." This wasn't the time to ask too many questions about the Menel. Riyannah was sharp enough to suspect he'd encountered the Menel before, and then she might be asking more questions about his travels than he could safely answer. She appeared to assume he'd come to Targa in another starship. Very good. As long as she went on assuming that, the Dimension X secret was safe.

"Life seemed good for all the people of all the stars," said Riyannah. "We and the Menel were at peace with each other and wished no one else any harm.

"Then we discovered Targa and Loyun Chard."

Targa was also a planet very much like Home Dimension Earth. Many centuries ago its civilization reached the point of nearly exhausting the planet's resources. A series of small conflicts grew into a thermonuclear war which killed half the people of Targa. Many of the survivors died of famine and disease. Civilization collapsed completely for over a century.

The Targans were tough, though. Enough of them survived to start up civilization again. Generation after generation, as the radioactivity died away, they rebuilt the cities, rediscovered lost science and technology, resettled the waste lands.

The one thing they could not do was recreate the resources the old civilization had used up. So the cities remained small and dependent on the countryside for food. The city people grew to hate this dependence and the farmers grew to exploit it, ruling the cities like tyrants. It was a situation which could only end in another war.

"At least there would have been another war, except for

63

Loyun Chard," said Riyannah. "He was good luck for the Targans."

Loyun Chard began as an officer in the air force of one of the cities. He overthrew the city's government, then led a brilliant airborne campaign against the farmers around the city. The farmers were routed, their lands were confiscated, and the city became truly independent.

With the prestige of his victory and his battle-hardened fighting men behind him, Loyun Chard was well launched on a career of conquest. One city after another came over to him and snatched its croplands from the men who farmed them. In ten years the farmers and country people were broken and Loyun Chard ruled most of Targa.

He was not only a conqueror, he was a farsighted statesman—at least from Targa's point of view. He gathered the most brilliant scientists and engineers, then turned them loose. Within a few years they discovered or invented practically everything necessary for spaceflight, including antigravity. Then someone playing around with the theories behind antigravity went on to discover the faster-than-light drive.

Suddenly the galaxy and all its resources lay open to Targa—and the Loyun Chard. "If he hadn't already been ambitious for further conquest, he certainly would have become so now," said Riyannah. "No one in the history of the old civilization had even conquered as much of Targa as he had. Now he could go on and make both his people and his name immortal."

Now there was a real prospect of unlimited resources and prosperity for all, or at least of new and rich planets to settle. It was obvious that no one who continued to fight against Loyun Chard would share in any of this. So opposition to Chard rapidly shrank. Within a few years he was able to disband much of his military strength and devote the resources to building his space fleet.

To be sure, he still kept some men under arms. An air force of jets patrolled the skies. Soldiers kept order in the conquered farmlands and occasionally rode the troop carriers into the wilderness on lightning raids.

The air force had only a few hundred planes, since oil to make fuel for the jets was rare and expensive. The antigravity devices which drove the spaceships were much too big and heavy to put into combat aircraft.

The soldiers had good weapons, but most of them were people who couldn't get any other job. They got little training, so they were heavy-footed and sometimes half-witted in the field. Without their air support, they would be much less of a menace.

In spite of these flaws, Chard's armed forces were strong enough to harry what was left of his opponents. Defections and defeats had driven them underground until Chard could probably have left the survivors to starve in the wilderness.

"He will not do this," said Riyannah. "He keeps the planes and men raiding to train them for the conquest of Kanan."

Blade frowned. Loyun Chard sounded like an ambitious, ruthless man, but hardly a raving maniac. It would take a maniac to plan the conquest of Kanan, if Riyannah's home planet was as she'd described it.

"Are you sure you aren't worrying unnecessarily?" he asked Riyannah. "How do you know he's planning to attack your world?"

Riyannah's voice was level. "He told us so himself."

Loyun Chard was getting his space program nicely underway when the Kananites and the Menel discovered Targa. The Targans reacted quite calmly to the arrival of visitors from outer space, and the Kananites couldn't help wondering why.

"The Menel flew into a panic when we first appeared in their skies," said Riyannah. "So why weren't the Targans doing the same? We soon found out. Loyun Chard was telling them that the conquest of Kanan would be an easy way to win the riches they hoped for."

"Did you make the same offer of scientific help you'd made to the Menel?" asked Blade.

"Yes. The Targans rejected it. Loyun Chard said that we were wretched, cowardly creatures who could not defend what we had. We were making our offer only out of fear, and perhaps in the hope of making Targa dependent on us. The true Targans, the destined master people, would never permit themselves to be dependent upon anyone. They would stride like giants across the stars, taking whatever they wanted from whoever held it."

"You're quoting him?" Loyun Chard's rhetoric had an

unpleasantly familiar ring. It reminded Blade of Adolf Hitler's ravings. The ravings of a madman—but Hitler had developed the resources to make those ravings into a terrible reality. Apparently Loyun Chard was doing the same.

Once Chard was sure he had his people behind him, Targan policy was shoot first and ask any necessary questions afterward. The two ships in orbit around Targa were captured, the Menel killed, and the Kananites taken down to the planet. They were tortured into revealing the location of Kanan, then publicly executed, and that was just the beginning.

The Kananites hadn't faced anything like this crisis since the first contact with the Menel, two hundred years before the oldest living Kananite was born. They not only didn't have any real knowledge of war, they weren't even sure how to go about acquiring that knowledge.

Eventually they decided to negotiate with the underground opposition to Chard, while Menel spaceships kept watch on the Targan space program. Not a bad plan, in theory. In practice, it ran into a few unexpected difficulties.

The opposition to Chard hated him as much as ever, since every one of them had friends and relatives to avenge. Unfortunately they were scattered and not well-armed. They were also more than a bit skeptical of the generosity of the Kananites with their technology.

"At times we thought we were still talking to Chard's men," Riyannah said wearily. "They wanted to know why—why—*why* we were giving them anything?"

"What did you tell them?"

"We said that with the knowledge we could give them, there would be no need to go out into space and loot other planets. They could do anything they needed with the resources of their own system."

"Perhaps that's true—" began Blade, but Riyannah interrupted him.

"Perhaps? You know it's true! Just for a start, they could make enough antigravity generators to put in all their planes, and then—"

"Yes, I know," said Blade patiently. "But are you sure they don't share Loyun Chard's dream of going out to the stars, even if they don't share his plans for what to do out there?"

Riyannah ignored Blade as if he hadn't spoken the last words and rushed on with her list of complaints against the Targan underground. Blade sighed. The Kananites not only needed to learn about war, they needed to learn about the fears and hopes of people who'd been fighting one for a generation. The underground had to be hard bargainers, suspicious of treachery and reluctant to be treated as poor relations. It sounded as if the Kananites were off on the wrong foot with them.

In any case, the Targan underground agreed in principle to aid Kanan against Chard in return for Kanan's energy technology. Like most agreements made "in principle," there were still a few dozen details to be worked out. Riyannah was a member of a delegation sent to cope with those details.

Meanwhile, Menel ships swooped low over Targa, trying to locate important targets. It quickly turned out that Menel spaceships couldn't survive against Chard's air force, let alone his spaceships. The Menel were brave enough and the hurd-ray was deadly, but Chard's pilots were far more skilled and their lasers and rockets more than good enough. At least twenty Menel ships were lost before the scouting flights stopped.

This was serious. The Kananites and the Menel only had about fifty armed spaceships, most of them small interplanetary patrol craft. All the rest of their ships were about as dangerous as a herd of dairy cows.

Eventually the Kananites and the Menel gave up trying to keep any sort of close watch on Targa. They set up a hidden base in the Targan system's asteroid belt and settled down to see what happened.

"I hope both your people and the Menel are at least building warships and training soldiers as fast as you can."

"I think we are converting a few ships for war. The Menel are doing the same. I do not know how many, though. The Menel are divided into Gorani—I do not know what your word is. Each Goran has a special task, and only the War Goran can fight or fly armed ships."

"Can't other Gorani of the Menel learn to fight?"

"No. It is not just a matter of law or custom. It is the way the Menel are raised from the time they are hatched.

One who is hatched and raised in one Goran cannot learn to do the work of another."

"I see." Blade didn't like what he saw but there was no point in mentioning it to Riyannah. The Menel seemed to be divided into a series of rigid classes. They were going to be seriously handicapped in a war with the more adaptable Targans.

"As for soldiers," Riyannah continued, "I cannot see how we will need them. If we can meet the Targans in space and keep them on their own planet, that will be enough. We don't need to conquer Targa. We don't even want to!" Her voice was almost shrill.

"I believe you, Riyannah," said Blade. "But you seem to have a problem with making your Targan friends believe it."

Riyannah sighed. "We certainly do."

Everything that could go wrong went wrong when Riyannah and five other Kananites came to Targa to negotiate with the underground. They were attacked from the air soon after leaving their spaceship in its hiding place. The leader of the delegation was badly hurt. Two others, including Riyannah, suffered head injuries sufficient to destroy their implanted knowledge of the Targan language.

"The Teacher Globes will teach you almost anything, including a language," she said. "But the knowledge does not go deeply into the brain. If you are drugged or hit on the head, you often forget what you've learned."

So that was what lay behind the maddening language problem! Lord Leighton's computer did its usual job on his brain, and the Teacher Globe no doubt did just as well for Riyannah. But sheer bad luck drove every word of Targan out of Riyannah's battered head!

A few days later, more planes attacked the underground camp where Riyannah and her comrades were hiding, smashing it completely. One of the Kananites and many of the underground's fighters were killed. The survivors had to flee across country, taking the wounded Kananite leader with them.

"The Targans soon saw how little we knew about life in the woods. That did not make them trust us more. Then our leader Marocah died, and we buried him in the forest, far from home." Riyannah was silent for a moment.

The fugitives eventually reached another underground

camp, and were finally able to open negotiations with the underground's leaders. These negotiations didn't get far. Perhaps Chard's men had tracked the fugitives, perhaps they were just lucky. In any case, the second camp was also attacked, both from the air and on the ground. Riyannah and a handful of people escaped just before the camp fell, to run into more soldiers as they tried to get clear.

That was where Blade came in, and after that he and Riyannah were partners in their adventures.

"We'd radioed to the asteroid base, and the two Menel ships you saw were on their way to pick us up. After they were destroyed, I knew I would have to return to the ship in the mountains to the north. It is so well hidden that I do not think Chard's men have found it. I trusted you not to kill me on the way, and after that—" She shrugged.

"Yes," said Blade. "And after that?"

"If I didn't think it was safe to take you to the asteroid base, I was going to kill you. I wasn't sure I could, but I knew I had to be ready to try. Even if I died, I could still send the ship to the asteroid on automatic control. What happened to us and what we'd learned had to get to the base."

What they'd learned was an important development in Loyun Chard's strategy. He was pouring material and manpower into building a monstrous starship nearly a mile long, heavily armed and armored, able to serve as a warship, exploration ship, and transport for colonists all at once.

"What it will do first is attack the asteroid base. It will certainly win, and the base will be destroyed. So will many of our ships and the Menel's, hundreds of our fighting people, and any hope of keeping the Targans in their own system. We will have to meet them out among the stars. The war will be far longer and more terrible if we must do that, and we may not win."

Loyun Chard no doubt knew that just as well as the Kananites. So he was building the great starship, *Dark Warrior*. The man was a formidable opponent, and peace would be in danger as long as he lived.

"If the two Menel ships hadn't fallen," said Riyannah, "we'd already be on the asteroid base, or even on our way to Kanan. With Menel to help me, I wouldn't have needed to kill you, no matter what."

69

"And now?"

Riyannah smiled and put her arms around him. "I think I can trust you to do nothing to help Loyun Chard. I do not know what else you may want to do, but if it is not dangerous to me or to Kanan, then it is your affair. I want to know more about you and your world, but you don't have to tell me if you don't want to."

"How did you come to trust me?"

"I knew you could not be my enemy after you saved me from the bat-cats. Before that—you were still a mystery. You'd saved my life and killed Targan soldiers. Yet you looked like a Targan, spoke Targan well, and kept me from helping the Menel."

"I did that to keep you from getting yourself killed, Riyannah."

"I know that now. I didn't at the time. Also, you didn't seem to understand who the Menel were. That meant you could not be one of the Targan underground fighters."

"And so I was a bigger mystery than before?" said Blade, stroking Riyannah's hair.

"Yes. Then the night after we came up the canyon, some of the mystery disappeared. I knew you could not be one of Loyun Chard's people."

"How was that?"

Riyannah laughed. "I got you to take off your clothes, then watched you. All of Chard's men have a lightning bolt tattooed on their penis, and a triangle on the inside of the right or the left thigh."

Blade stiffened, put both hands on Riyannah's shoulders, and held her at arm's length.

"A lightning bolt tattooed on the penis?"

"Yes. Down the middle. The officers have the triangle on the inside of the right thigh, the ordinary soldiers on the—"

"Riyannah, what are you—?"

"I'm telling you the truth, Blade. If you'd looked at the bodies of the soldiers, you'd have seen it for yourself."

Blade nodded slowly. "A tattoo on the penis," he said, half to himself. Then he threw his head back and roared with laughter until the echoes rolled around the forest.

"A tattoo on the penis," he gasped, tears running down his cheeks. "*A tattoo on the penis!*" Then he reached out for Riyannah again, and she came into his arms. He felt her lips on his and her hands fumbling at his trousers. He thrust his hands inside the back of her trousers and cupped her buttocks. She laughed and tossed her head so that her hair brushed his face and neck.

Then all the delicious sensations of making love to Riyannah were coming so fast Blade could no longer sort them out.

Chapter 10

Toward dawn Riyannah fell asleep. Blade wanted to but found he couldn't. His mind was still whirling too fast from what Riyannah told him. She'd answered some of his questions, but left many others open and raised some completely new ones.

The most important question was also the least easily answered. Was she telling the truth? If she wasn't, what if Blade went with her to Kanan? He might be signing his own death warrant, as well as helping the wrong side in a war. He would be alone, against the resources of a whole planet. He could be eliminated as easily as a swatted mosquito—more easily, if they didn't teach him the Kananite language.

That wasn't the only problem he might face if he went to Kanan and found its people hostile. So far Riyannah seemed to believe his story about being the survivor of a wrecked spaceship. What about the Kananites back home? With the resources of their home planet, they might probe his brain, prove he was lying, reveal the truth, and perhaps even discover the Dimension X secret. Then what? Blade had a vision of the Kananites unleashed on the whole universe, like the Looters who'd also discovered inter-Dimensional travel and used it to destroy one civilization after another until Blade met and defeated them in Tharn.

Even assuming the Kananites didn't get the Dimension X secret, they still might get the location of Earth from him. Then a swarm of Menel and Kananite ships might descend on Earth, drawing it into a Kananite empire.

So much for what could happen if Riyannah was lying. There wasn't much he could hope to do against it, except keep alert and be ready to put himself out of reach of the Kananites. He doubted they could get much out of a corpse.

72

What if Riyannah was telling the truth? It would probably be safe to go to Kanan, although the less they learned about Dimension X the better. After that, what he ought to do would depend on the answer to another maddening question.

Where was he? Had he been hurled across the Dimensions to an alternate Earth, so that none of the people here could be any menace to Home Dimension as long as they could only travel in space? Or was he on another world in the same Dimension as the Earth he knew, separated from it only by light-years of space? He remembered the moment of cold and star-studded blackness all around him. Was that a leap between Dimensions, or across light-years within a single Dimension?

Just to make things more confusing, what about the other two times he'd met the Menel? Why had he now met them three times in three different Dimensions, or worlds, or whatever? What had happened to him the other two times? Did the Menel perhaps have the ability to travel among the Dimensions and hadn't told the Kananites?

Blade laughed softly. As far as finding out where he was, talking to Riyannah hadn't helped at all. If he got back to Home Dimension with this load of mysteries, Lord Leighton was going to drop dead from sheer frustration at so many unanswerable questions!

If he got back. Soberly Blade faced that unpleasant little word. If Lord Leighton's computer had twisted space as well as his senses, hurling him across light-years, could it reach out and grip his brain as usual? Or was this going to be a one-way trip into wherever he'd ended up?

Blade decided to call it Wherever instead of Dimension X until he knew a little more. The only way to learn that little more was to go with Riyannah to Kanan. The underground people couldn't help him. Loyun Chard's people would almost certainly kill him, whether or not they could be any danger to Home Dimension Earth. Out among the stars he might find a greater treasure than he'd ever found before, the treasure of Kanan's scientific knowledge.

A great weight seemed to lift from Blade's mind with this decision. Part of the relief was simply knowing what came next. Another part was knowing that he'd be traveling on with Riyannah. They'd been through too much together for him to feel comfortable about leaving her.

After breakfast that morning, Blade asked Riyannah how far it was to her spaceship.

"About three or four days, if we walk as fast as you like to." She wrinkled up her face in comic dismay at the idea.

"I'm afraid we'd better walk that fast, Riyannah. Chard's planes might be searching for the ship."

"It won't be easy for them to find it. We have it hidden well inside a cave at the foot of the Mount Grolin. The mountain has three peaks, so it's easy to recognize."

The slopes of a high mountain would give little cover from Chard's air force, but it couldn't be helped. "You can fly the ship yourself?"

"Oh yes. It practically flies itself, and all of us who came in it learned how to handle it. But it will help if you can manage the hurd-ray controls."

"I should be able to do that. I was in charge of the weapons aboard my ship."

"Are you of the War Goran of your people?"

"No. We are not like the Menel. We prefer to have each of our people able to learn to fight."

"Like the Targans?" said Riyannah quietly.

"I do not think we have much else in common with the Targans. Many years ago, a man like Loyun Chard tried to conquer our world. We fought a terrible war to stop him. In the end he was defeated and killed himself. We don't care for people like Loyun Chard. So I am coming with you to Kanan to help you fight him. Now let's stop talking and start packing."

They were on the move by noon, taking only what they needed for the march. The load was still enough to make Riyannah grunt as she slung on her pack, but she was smiling as she picked up her rifle. She was on her way home, however rough and long the road might be. Blade wished he could be so cheerful.

After a while he was. It was a beautiful day, just cool enough to keep them both comfortable, with the sun striking golden through the leaves. Once Riyannah stopped to pick some blue flowers and stick them in her silvery hair. There was always a bird singing somewhere nearby, and Blade found it almost too easy to forget this wasn't a picnic or a vacation.

They slept that night in their blankets, curled together for warmth, rifles in hand. In the morning they refilled their canteens from a spring and Blade climbed a tree to study the route ahead. He thought he saw a mountain with three peaks far off to the northwest, but couldn't be sure.

That evening he climbed another tree, and this time the three-peaked mountain stood out unmistakably. When he described it to Riyannah, she almost danced with delight.

"That has to be Mount Grolin!" she said. "There's nothing else like it. If you can see what you've seen, we'll be there the day after tomorrow!"

Riyannah was right. They hadn't gone far on the fourth day before the trees began to thin out. By noon they had the three snowcapped peaks of Mount Grolin continuously in sight. By mid-afternoon they were out on the bare mountainside, with nothing growing around them but wiry grass and gray-blue lichens. If the spaceship was much higher, they'd have to spend a night in the open without the warm clothing they'd need.

At least the ground ahead offered plenty of cover. It was rugged and scarred, with enough boulders and ravines to hide a small army. It would be rough going, but it would also take a lot of luck for a pilot to spot them.

They spent the night huddled in the shelter of a boulder. Blade stuffed handfuls of lichen into their boots for extra insulation, and somehow they managed to not only survive but even sleep. They both woke feeling stiff, half numb, and generally wretched, but the first few hundred yards of climbing thawed them out and limbered them up.

A mile farther on, they spotted the enemy camp.

Fortunately they spotted it from a particularly rugged stretch of mountainside, one where Blade would have been glad to have some climbing gear. Taking off his pack and boots, he crawled silently forward until he could get a good look at the camp. Then he returned to Riyannah.

"It could be worse. I saw only one complete shelter. They must still be setting the camp up. I don't think there will be more than twenty soldiers."

Riyannah tried to smile, not very successfully. "Do you think this camp means they've found the ship?"

"I don't know. Did you put any traps or weapons at the mouth of the cave to stop anyone trying to get in?"

Riyannah shook her head. "We don't have anything like

75

that on Kanan. We haven't needed it," she added in reply to Blade's frown.

Blade shook his head slowly. He was going to have problems on Kanan even if the people were friendly. The Kananites seemed to be rather naive and innocent when it came to the practical little details of war. This wasn't necessarily a vice, just as his own skill in killing wasn't always a virtue. Right now, though, the Kananites' innocence could mean victory for Loyun Chard.

"Since we can't know if they've found the ship, we'll have to go on. Where on the mountain is the cave?"

"You can't see it from here," said Riyannah. "It's just around the ridge of the peak farthest to the east. There's a streak of black rock running down from the summit. The cave is at the bottom of the streak."

"All right," said Blade. "We'll swing wide around the camp to the west. The ground to the east is too flat to hide us. We should still get to the foot of the mountain by midnight. Then a few hours' sleep, and we can make a final push just after dawn. Think you can make it?"

"It would be foolish to give up now, when we're so close," said Riyannah. She started to get to her feet.

Blade said nothing, but he didn't like the weariness in her voice or on her face. Her lips were cracked and her eyes were red, with great dark circles around them. As he gripped her shoulders to help her up, Blade could feel her shivering.

They'd covered more than half the distance to the foot of the mountain when Blade stiffened and pushed Riyannah behind a rock. Then he lay down, rifle ready and eyes searching the sky toward the Targan camp.

The whirring sound he'd heard grew louder, and the dot he'd seen in the distant sky took shape. It was one of Chard's troop carriers, heading straight for the camp. Blade waited until it landed and the dust raised by the propellers settled. Then he crept behind the boulder and told Riyannah what he'd seen and what it meant.

She stiffened as if he'd jabbed her with a needle and one hand clenched until the nails drew blood from the palm. "We'll have to go straight on to the cave," she said. "I notice you've been staying where the rocks hide us. Well, there aren't any rocks like that around the foot of the mountain. It's all smooth and open there. The climb up to the cave is even worse."

Blade nodded, realizing what Riyannah was trying to say. They couldn't risk crossing a wide stretch of open ground in daylight, not now. If they kept moving all night, though, they'd be crossing the open ground under cover of darkness. They'd be much harder to see.

Except—

"What about you, Riyannah? The cold's already getting to you, isn't it? Can you survive a night march?"

"If we get to the ship, I'll be all right. The cabin is warm, and there will be food and hot drinks."

"We may not have time to prepare any food. With that troop carrier around—"

"There are some drugs too. They'll do everything that's needed." She lurched to her feet, and they were off again.

Afterward, Blade would have given a good deal to be able to forget that night's march across the mountainside. Unfortunately most of the details stuck in his memory and would not leave.

The slow gnawing of the cold at his fingers and toes, turning them first into burning twigs, then taking away all feeling.

Riyannah's face turning paler and more pinched with each passing mile, until there was nothing alive in her face except the great eyes staring ahead.

His own breath freezing on his dirt-caked beard, until he could see a layer of silver-white frost over the dark hair. The frost seemed to be exactly the same color as Riyannah's hair.

Riyannah's stumbling and falling, and his holding her feet against his stomach until enough warmth crept back into them for her to move on.

The chill light of the stars and the crescent moon, and the warm orange glow of the lights of the Targan camp. There were moments when Blade could almost imagine those lights were distant campfires where he and Riyannah could find warmth and comfort. Then the effort of taking another step would snap his mind out of the fantasy.

In the end that was what kept him and Riyannah going—taking that one more step, another after that, then still another. Blade knew that if they didn't keep moving,

it would all be over within a few minutes. They were stag-
gering along in summer clothes through temperatures that
couldn't be far above zero.

They were still on their feet and still moving when the
eastern sky began to turn pale. By the time the dawn was
pink and the camp's lights went out, they were within sight
of the streak of black rock.

The mountain dawn was beautiful, but there wasn't
much warmth in it and Blade was too cold to appreciate
beauty. He couldn't remember when he'd last felt his fingers or toes, and vaguely wondered if the ship's medicine
chest had any remedies for frostbite. Then he felt Riyannah's hand clutch his shoulder, and turned to see her raise
the other hand and point upward.

"There it is." Blade saw a faint line of shadow in the
dark rock.

"It looks too small. You're sure?"

"Yes. The cave—makes a bend inside the mouth—gets
wider." Riyannah shaped each word slowly and painfully,
as if she was carving them out of the ice. Then she turned
toward the cave and stepped ahead of Blade. He put out a
hand to steady her. As he did, the silent dawn was shat-
tered by the swelling roar of jets.

There were three of the flying disks, and they swung out
from between the peaks of Mount Grolin in a slow turn.
They had plenty of time to scan the slopes below them—
and see the two figures silhouetted against the snow.

Blade's hopes that the planes hadn't seen them vanished
as one of them peeled off from the formation and swept
down toward them. Flame winked under its nose and
snow spurted up a hundred yards downslope from them.
As the plane pulled out of its dive, Blade saw the undersides of the wings. The weapons racks were empty. As the
other two planes came in, he saw the same was true with
them.

As the roar of the guns died away, Blade raised his
head and shouted to Riyannah, "Run! Get into the cave
and start up the ship. I'll stay out here and give them a
target."

"Richard—"

"Damn it, get moving! If you're on the black rock before they come in again, they may not see you!"

Riyannah stared at him for a moment that to Blade's

78

distorted senses seemed to last an hour. Then she kissed him, two pairs of half-frozen lips meeting numbly. She turned, unharnessed her pack, tossed Blade her rifle, and scrambled furiously toward the black rock.

Blade watched her reach it. Then he saw the planes coming in and turned to face them—one man with two rifles and a handful of grenades against three jet fighters.

Chapter 11

On their second pass the planes laid down three lines of fire, parallel like the tines of a fork. Smoke and snow, rock fragments and ricocheting pieces of metal sprayed in all directions. Blade couldn't have seen to aim at the planes, even if he'd dared stand up.

As the planes banked away, Blade looked up the black rock toward the mouth of the cave. He could barely make out a small figure scuttling upward, now less than a hundred feet from the cave mouth. If he could barely see Riyannah, the pilots could hardly spot her as they flew past at four hundred miles an hour.

Blade quickly pulled Riyannah's ammunition out of her pack and stuffed it into his own. Then he slung her rifle across his back and rammed a fresh magazine into his own. The five grenades were in a pouch on his hip.

The howl of jets swelled again. Two of the planes were coming at him while a third seemed to be hanging back, aiming off to one side. Blade's breath caught in his throat as he saw the line of flying snow leap toward the black rock. Then he breathed again as it crossed the rock a hundred yards above the cave mouth. He looked for Riyannah, saw her crawling up the last few yards of steep rock just below the cave, and a warmth he hadn't felt in many hours flowed through him. Before the planes could come in again she'd be safe inside the cave.

The burst of fire from the other two planes was shorter this time but also closer. Blade felt rock dust and driven snow blast his exposed skin, while something larger drilled through his trousers into his thigh. It felt like a dozen wasps stinging him at once, and as he rolled over he saw blood soaking through torn cloth.

As Blade rolled, he saw that one of the planes would pass directly over him only a couple of hundred feet up.

He continued to roll until the rifle was pointing at the sky, then squeezed down on the trigger. Jet planes were full of fragile moving parts in this or any other Dimension. Rifle fire could bring them down and often had.

Blade couldn't have aimed better if he'd been using a radar-directed antiaircraft gun. The plane flew straight into the burst of heavy slugs. Suddenly the smoke coming from one engine was heavy and black. It flew away without trying to turn, and now smoke was coming from the belly as well as the engine. It started to turn, leaving a black smoke trail like an immense question mark scrawled across the blue sky. The other two planes banked, trying to stay with it.

Then suddenly one whole wing and the belly were blotted out by greasy black smoke. A torch of orange flame licked through the smoke. Then the plane pulled up, the sun glinted on the canopy as it flew off, and white smoke gushed out of the cockpit. Two dark shapes soared out of the smoke, the pilots in rocket-boosted ejection seats. Then the plane's nose rose still higher, it stalled, whipped into a tight spiral, and plunged down toward the mountainside.

Snow, smoke, flame, and flying wreckage erupted where it struck. A gray-black fog spread half a mile wide, cutting off Blade's view of the camp. Above the smoke the white canopies of two parachutes blossomed, as the pilots pulled their ripcords and started their drift down to safety. One plane down should throw a scare into the others and gain some precious time.

Before the smoke cleared, Blade dashed across the bullet-pocked snow and scrambled up onto the black rock. The best cover he could find there was less than two feet high, but that should gain him still more time. When the Targans got close enough to see him against the rock, they'd be within easy range.

Now the troop carrier was lifting out from the camp. It hugged the ground all the way to the foot of Mount Grolin, then landed about half a mile from Blade. He strained his eyes, trying to count the men climbing out and forming a skirmish line. It was hard to be sure, but he thought there were only about a dozen. Were they leaving some to hold the camp, or—?

The carrier took off again. Instead of climbing it

hovered low as the men on the ground began their advance up the mountainside. Now Blade could count them more accurately. Definitely fewer than a dozen, and where were the rest? Blade began to wonder what the Targans might be planning. His thoughts grew unpleasant as the carrier came closer and he saw the guns in its nose and side doors.

Now the men on the ground were only a quarter of a mile away—rifle range for someone who had plenty of ammunition. The Targans did. Blade didn't. He tried to hunch down even lower behind his cover, kept his eyes on the carrier, and wondered what was keeping Riyannah.

Then the carrier was climbing. It swept past Blade to the left, and he could see the door facing him crowded with helmeted heads. He could have hit it easily, but the number of guns sticking out of it kept him frozen in place. He realized what the Targans were up to.

They were going to hit him from both above and below. The men on the ground were already in position to shoot if he showed himself. Now the carrier was going to drop the others upslope from him. Then they'd work their way down the mountain until they could hit him from behind—and also hit the mouth of the cave.

Blade knew he had to move up to the cave now, when it would be just risky instead of suicidal. He had to last as long as possible, to keep all the Targans as far as possible from the cave. They'd certainly have weapons which could cripple the ship at close range.

As for his own chances of getting out of here, they hardly seemed worth considering. It looked like a question of how many Targans he was going to kill first and not much else.

Blade rose to a crouch and dashed upward, zigzagging wildly. Someone in the carrier spotted movement, and so did someone below. A laser beam from the carrier crackled down fifty yards to Blade's left, turning snow into steam. A rocket soared up from the men on the ground, sailed clean over Blade's head, and went off just above the mouth of the cave with a *kwumpph* and a cloud of green smoke. It hit close enough to the carrier to rock it. Blade could almost hear the curses as the men in the door struggled to keep from being pitched out on the rock be-

82

low. The carrier's next laser beam went so wide Blade could barely see it.

Blade kept moving but felt a little better. If the Targans got nervous enough about hitting each other, it might slow them down a little more. Time, time, *time!* Damn it, Riyannah, you don't have all day to get that ship moving!

As the carrier moved out of their line of fire, the men on the ground opened up with their rifles. Bullets and an occasional rocket hit all around the mouth of the cave. Someone down there must have realized Blade was heading for it. If Riyannah stuck her ship's nose out of the cave and straight into a rocket—

A high-pitched whine tore at Blade's ears, louder than the whine of the jets and far more painful. He clutched the rifle, although he wanted to drop it and clap his hands over his ears.

The ground shuddered. Chunks of rock and ice spewed out of the cave mouth like shot from the muzzle of a gigantic shotgun. The shockwave tore through the air and knocked Blade flat. He fell on top of the rifle and rolled to bring it back to firing position. As he did, Riyannah's spaceship swept out of the cave.

It looked like a fat silvery tadpole, fifty feet from nose to tail. A small canopy was perched on the nose and a hurd-ray projector stuck out of the belly. The projector swiveled, crimson fire sprayed the mountainside, and the soldiers below disappeared in smoke and steam. Their screams were loud enough to penetrate even Blade's half-deafened ears.

Then the ship was drifting toward him, the air shimmering blue around its tail, a hatch open in its belly. A metallic cord with a handgrip on the end unwound itself from the hatch and struck the ground yards from Blade. He dropped his rifle and lunged for it. He barely had time to take a firm grip before the ship rose again. For several long seconds he dangled in midair, bullets whistling past below him, feeling like the daring young man on the flying trapeze and hoping Riyannah would remember to reel him in.

Then the cord jerked up violently and Blade flew in through the hatch, slamming down on the floor hard enough to knock the wind out of him. The hatch clanged shut behind him and the floor tilted wildly. Blade went head over heels and crashed into a bulkhead. "Riyannah!" he shouted. "Get this crate under control or let me get to a seat! You're going to splatter me all over the place!"

If anything the ship climbed more steeply, but Blade heard an enormously refreshing sound—Riyannah's laughter. Then:

"All right. I'll level off, but hurry! The other two planes are coming after us!"

Blade practically leaped through the door in front of him. On the other side was a compartment about fifteen feet square and eight feet high. Padded seats took up most of the floor and control consoles most of the front end. Riyannah was perched on a high seat in the middle, head thrust up through the canopy and hands resting on a small black box suspended from the roof of the compartment. She was stark naked except for a silver G-string and sandals, her hair tossed wildly, and Blade could have sworn her green eyes were glowing. For a member of a peaceful race she looked astoundingly warlike, a silver-haired goddess of battle.

As Blade dropped into the nearest seat the ship lurched violently. Riyannah jumped and said something, probably unprintable, in the Kananite language. Several of the consoles glowed all the colors of the rainbow, and from aft Blade heard a noise like a toilet backing up.

Riyannah cursed again and pointed to a console with something like a radar screen over it and a face-covering helmet hung beside the screen. "Blade, take the hurd-ray. We've been hit and it's all I can do to control the ship!"

"How do you—?"

"Put on the helmet, turn on the screen, and look at it. When you're looking straight at the plane on the screen, a red light will go on. Push the button under the red light."

Blade vaulted into the seat nearest the console and snatched up the helmet. The ship took another hit as he pulled it on, and the jolt nearly made him cut off an ear with the edge of the helmet. Then the ship swung in a tight circle, squashing Blade down into the seat. One of the Targan planes appeared on the screen. He stared at it, saw the light go on, and pushed the button.

The screen glowed crimson as the hurd-ray fired, then it was blotted out by smoke and flying wreckage as the plane exploded. Riyannah let out a banshee's scream and Blade's own roar of triumph echoed her.

Then Riyannah flung herself backward in her seat. Blade had just time to imitate her. Then acceleration flattened him into his seat until he thought his bones were going to collapse and let his flesh and internal organs spread like jam.

How long the acceleration lasted, Blade never found out. He only knew that it eventually came to an end. As he drifted back to full awareness he realized he was floating against the straps of his seat. The ship was clear of Targa and plunging out into space in free fall. The screen he'd used to aim the hurd-ray showed nothing but blackness and a few stars.

Riyannah was floating around the cabin, still wearing only the G-string and sandals. Her eyes half-shut and dull, but she pulled herself briskly down to look at Blade. When she'd satisfied herself he was all right, she drifted over to one of the panels and began pushing buttons.

"I've got to drop the power plant," she said. "The Targans hit it too often, and it will become unstable in a few more minutes."

Blade found he could speak. "What are we going to use for power?"

"We're already on a course that will take us within radio range of the asteroid belt. The patrol ship will come out to get us when they pick up our radio signals."

"What about the Targan ships?"

"We're traveling too fast for anything except *Dark Warrior* herself to catch us. Even if they could come after us, they'll think we blew up when the power plant explodes." She punched a complicated sequence of buttons. Something clicked under the floor and something else rang like a great bell in the tail of the ship. The jolt threw Blade against his straps.

Now Riyannah pulled something pistol-shaped out of a drawer under one console and began running it through her hair. As she did she revolved gently in midair. Blade saw that in spite of her cheerful, brisk manner, the last few days had left their marks on her. The red-brown skin was dark with bruises in half a dozen places and seemed stretched even more tightly than before over her delicate bones. She must be running on nerves and drugs, and per-

85

haps also on the happiness of being back in a familiar place, safely on the way home.

Riyannah had just finished cleaning her hair when a soundless explosion of raw light burst on the screen, flooding the cabin. Half-dazzled, Blade reached out for Riyannah's hand and felt her fingers close on his wrist. Lying side by side, Riyannah in midair and Blade still strapped in his seat, they watched the screen.

Far behind them an expanding globe of purple fire hung in space fading slowly. Sparks of red and gold trailed out of it to drift off into the blackness. It was something as violent as an atomic explosion but definitely not the same. That purple glow was fading too slowly. Some sort of energy-generating reaction was still going on back there, minutes after the explosion. Blade watched the purple glow shrink and fade, still throwing out sparks. Then he could see the planet they were leaving behind, and he instantly lost interest in the explosion.

Targa was—Earth. There was a little more dust in the atmosphere, so the clouds were more gray than white and the outlines of the continents weren't always clear. That was a minor detail. Everything else Blade could see, down to the smallest cape and bay, was what he'd seen in photographs of Earth taken from space.

It was a big universe, and no doubt it was possible that somewhere a planet existed which could look this much like Earth. Such a planet was only a theory, though, and Dimension X was a fact. Blade knew he'd been shifted sideways through the Dimension, not across light-years of space to another world in the same Dimension. That was the only reasonable explanation now. Targa and Kanan and the Menel were fighting their interstellar war across the light-years in Dimension X.

That thought was awesome, but it was also something of a relief. It was awesome, because it implied that each Dimension was a whole universe, not just a whole Earth. It implied an infinity of infinities, an idea even Lord Leighton might have some difficulty grasping.

It was also a relief to know that he was in Dimension X. He'd made it home from some weird places before, and it would be an unpleasant surprise if he couldn't make it home from Targa. Not from Kanan—he still wasn't sure the computer could reach across both Dimensions and light-years—but if he could somehow get back to Targa he should be all right.

Meanwhile he could help Kanan or refuse to help them without worrying about what they might do to Earth. Unless they got the whole Dimension X secret as well as their interstellar drive, Home Dimension Earth was as far beyond their reach as anything could be. He'd still have to guard the Dimension X secret, but that was a simpler proposition than what he'd been facing before.

Blade looked at the screen again. Before Riyannah dumped the power plant, it must have given the ship a terrific velocity. Targa was distinctly smaller than when he'd first seen it. The outlines of the continents were beginning to blur and the planet was turning into a cloud-flecked blue ball.

Riyannah was now strapped into her seat again, and from the regular rise and fall of her breasts Blade realized she was asleep. In sleep her face relaxed, all the strain and tension gone along with the warrior-goddess look.

She'd said the Kananites were peaceful, with no wars for a thousand years. Perhaps she was shading the truth. Or perhaps Riyannah was not quite typical of her people. Certainly there was a warrior in Riyannah, and not far below the surface either. She had courage, common sense, the ability to enjoy a good fight, and the ability to pick up technical details quickly.

That was enough to make a warrior and even a war leader. More than enough, considering how senseless and slow to learn some of history's "great captains" had been. If there were more Kananites like Riyannah, the Targans might not have an easy victory, or indeed any victory at all.

Blade yawned, tightened the straps to keep from floating around the cabin, and drifted off to sleep himself.

Chapter 12

Blade awoke to find Riyannah floating in the air in front of him. She was holding onto the arm of his seat with one hand and rubbing his thigh with a soft cloth held in the other. He saw that he was now naked, while Riyannah was wearing a loose coverall with a closing strip from throat to groin.

"Lie still a little more, Richard. You shouldn't have gone to sleep without looking at that wound. I had to do more to get out the infection than I should have. I'm not a doctor, you know."

He patted her free hand. "I know. But I seem to remember a certain lady who also fell asleep as if she'd been hit on the head."

Riyannah pulled a small black tube from a pouch at her belt and sprayed something cool and scented on Blade's thigh. Then she let go of the seat and sat cross-legged in midair in front of him.

"I did sleep. The drugs I used to fight the cold and get ready to fly the ship wouldn't last forever. If I tried to go on, I'd be sick, starting with my stomach. Have you ever taken a long trip in a spaceship with no gravity after someone has been sick to their stomach?"

Blade considered the idea and nodded. "I see what you mean." He sat up and reached out to pull Riyannah toward him, but she kicked herself just out of reach. "No, Richard. Right now I think we eat."

Blade realized that his stomach was too empty even to rumble and nodded again. "Yes. I'm going to enjoy something beside Targan emergency rations and half-raw meat for a change."

Riyannah set an alarm so they'd be warned if the radar set picked up any other ships. "I think we're too far out

88

for the Targans and too close to Targa for any of our own. But you never know."

"What will we do without the power plant if a Targan ship does find us?"

"We should be moving too fast for it to even hit us. We can also shoot back a few times with the hurd-ray, using the emergency power cells. After that——" She shrugged, a motion which made her body twist sensuously in the zero gravity.

The meal was dried and frozen foods mixed with hot water or thawed in a small infrared oven. There was a meat that tasted like a cross between turkey and ham, something like mashed potatoes with a delicious nutty flavor, and three kinds of vegetables which looked and tasted like nothing Blade had ever imagined. Dessert was a crunchy blue-fleshed fruit, soaked in something like highly spiced honey. Riyannah prepared enough food for six people but there were no leftovers.

After dinner Riyannah opened the refrigerator and brought out three frost-covered green bottles. With a little suction pump she filled two plastic bulbs from one of the bottles, shoved a straw into each one, and handed one to Blade.

The drink that came out when Blade squeezed the bulb looked like turpentine but tasted like a rich, well-aged sweet wine. It was certainly powerful. By the time Blade was sure he had the knack of drinking from the bulbs, he was beginning to feel it.

Riyannah emptied one bulb in a few minutes, went through a second nearly as fast, and started on a third. By the time she'd finished that third, her speech was slurred, she giggled, she floated on her back with arms and legs trailing loosely. Blade could have believed she was simply getting happily drunk to celebrate their escape if he hadn't seen her face when she thought he wasn't looking at her.

There were too many memories for Riyannah in this cabin, memories of the last time she'd been in it, bound for Targa with her comrades. Had she been in love with one of them? Certainly they'd been on their way to Targa with high hopes of an alliance with the underground and victory over Loyun Chard.

Now she was returning in a crippled ship, leaving her friends dead on Targa. She was returning with a man of another race who'd become friend, lover, and trusted comrade in battle, but how much was he really worth? She was also returning without an alliance with the underground and with news of the deadly threat of *Dark Warrior*. She'd failed and she wanted to forget both the failure and her dead friends.

Riyannah pushed the empty bottle away from her. It clinked against the ceiling and drifted off as she reached for another. Before she could open the new bottle, Blade was beside her. He pressed one hand gently into the small of her back to hold her against him. With the other hand he opened her coveralls. Then his lips were on her breasts, kissing, stroking, drawing her nipples out into hard points. She sighed and her arms locked around his back, her hands pressing into his buttocks. Blade's lips moved down to the flat stomach, she moaned, her legs wrapped around his hips—

By the time they slept again, Riyannah's skin was covered with a gleaming layer of sweat. She lolled bonelessly in the air, eyes closed and all the lines gone from her face.

Blade hoped they'd stay away.

They quickly established a regular cycle of eating, sleeping, lovemaking, housekeeping, and conversation. Each complete cycle they called a "day," since they had no other way of telling the time in the eternal sunlight of outer space.

Blade found that making love in zero gravity was even more complicated than he'd expected. There were certainly advantages to it. They could fall asleep still locked together, then wake without muscles cramped or arms and legs fallen asleep. They could also make love without worrying about whose weight would be on whom. This was important, considering that Blade weighed nearly twice as much as Riyannah.

On the other hand, there were certain problems. Some of them were rather exotic. For example, how do you handle the normal muscular contractions of orgasm, which will send both partners into a slow cartwheel around the cabin until they bump into something?

Solving this and other problems was amusing, but also sometimes a bit exhausting. Once after they'd bumped their heads on the ceiling for the third time in one day, Blade raised a question.

"Maybe we'd better strap ourselves down the next time?"

Riyannah frowned. "I suppose we could," she said thoughtfully. "But would that be as much fun?"

"You're right."

They spent several hours each day talking of their home worlds. Blade described a Home Dimension Earth a little more advanced scientifically and a good deal less divided and warlike. This saved him the trouble and risk involved in making up everything as he went along.

The strain of spinning these tales sometimes gave Blade sleepless hours. He didn't want to lie to Riyannah. He was sure he wouldn't have to, if everything was up to the two of them. But neither of them was their own master. If he told Riyannah the truth, could he trust her not to tell other Kananites who might take advantage of the information? Probably not. Then what would happen to him if the Kananites decided they should try ripping the Dimension X secret out of him?

Blade had still another reason for leaving out some of the uglier details of Home Dimension Earth. Riyannah said that the Kananites had outlawed war a thousand years ago. What would she think of an account of World War II? She might understand why Blade was willing to help stop Loyun Chard, the Hitler of Targa. She might also think Blade came from a race of bloodthirsty maniacs. What would happen then?

On the tenth day they picked up a radio signal that Riyannah said came from a patrol ship. On the twelfth day they were able to reply and exchange messages. Two days after that a Menel-crewed patrol ship matched courses with them and took them aboard. There was no way to salvage their crippled ship, so she was allowed to continue on course. In time she would leave the Targan system entirely and become another derelict wandering endlessly through the freezing emptiness of interstellar space.

Three days more traveling brought them to the asteroid base.

Chapter 13

It took Blade quite a while to get used to the sights at the asteroid base.

The base took up most of the asteriod, an oval chunk of rock about twenty miles long and twelve miles thick. Most of it was a mass of workshops, spaceship hangars, laboratories and observatories, and living quarters. Everything was connected by a maze of tunnels and elevators. About two-thirds of the asteroid was strictly out of bounds to Blade.

In the very center of the asteroid was an artificial cave a mile and a half wide and a thousand feet high. The floor of the cave was a carefully tended park, with flowers, lawns, full-sized trees, and even a small lake.

Scattered through the park were dozens of buildings of as many different shapes, sizes, and uses. Blade saw buildings made of brick, metal, wood, and plastic. He saw a few whose walls weren't even solid matter, but shimmering golden force fields. He saw shops, restaurants, public baths, athletic fields, and secluded vine-grown pavilions for open-air lovemaking.

Everywhere he saw both Kananites and Menel moving about and mingling freely, with less strain than he'd seen between tourists and local people in Paris or London. Kananites drifted into Menel-owned shops and came out with small bottles of brown powder that Riyannah said were spices. Menel either stood at tables or lay on couches —since they could not sit in Kananite-owned restaurants— using three-tined forks to demolish huge plates of fried vegetables and emptying copper steins of what looked like pink beer.

Eventually Blade got used to ducking flying claws when Menel got into particularly heated arguments. He got used to pointing out items on a menu to a waiter who looked like an eight-foot stalk of asparagus and held a computerized notepad in a foot-long claw like a lobster's. He even got used to telling when one of the Menel had drunk more than he could handle.

"It doesn't happen very often," said Riyannah. "Their systems can absorb so much alcohol that they usually get indigestion before they get drunk. But sometimes one has a—a 'cast-iron stomach,' you call it?"

"Yes."

"Then it—"

"It?"

"Yes. The Menel are neuter except when they want to reproduce, and they never do that except on their home planet."

"Do they avoid sex when they're neuter?"

"Oh no, the external organs still function. They just have a different set of rituals and techniques." Riyannah hesitated. "In fact, their organs are physically compatible with Kananite sex organs. Some of the more—curious—of both races have developed methods for sex with each other."

Blade tried hard to imagine what that must look like and failed completely. He also hoped he wouldn't have to try interspecies sex in order to be accepted among either the Kananites or the Menel. He was a fairly broad-minded and experienced man, but he did have his limits.

"I think we were talking about liquor, not sex," he said to Riyannah. "So the Menel sometimes get drunk. Then what happens?"

"Sometimes they just fall asleep. The rest of the time—if you ever see a Menel walking and holding himself absolutely straight and rigid, keep out of its way. When they drink they stop swaying."

"Unlike my people, who start swaying when they've had too much to drink," said Blade. They were sitting in an outdoor cafe, and he divided the last of a bottle of wine between his cup and Riyannah's.

"Kananites too," said Riyannah, running her hand up his arm to his shoulder. "Shall we sway off somewhere together and find a nice quiet patch of grass?"

"Sounds like a damned good idea," said Blade. That was the end of a serious conversation for several hours.

The Menel and the Kananites seemed to have worked

out a fairly complete system of sign language, allowing for the physical differences between them. The Menel had no fingers, but they did have two extra arms. Blade saw entire meals ordered and large purchases made in shops without a single word or sound.

Every so often, though, Menel and Kananites wanted to conduct more detailed conversations, for business or pleasure or simple curiosity. Then they needed help.

Every hundred yards or so all over the central cave were clusters of red globes perched on green poles. Each globe had a set of dials and buttons on each side, as well as earplugs and microphones hung on hooks. When a Menel and a Kananite wanted to talk, they found a vacant globe, stepped up to opposite sides, and put on the earplugs and microphones. Then they would settle down for anything from a few minutes to a few hours, taking turns listening and talking.

Some of the globes stood alone. Most were in clusters of four to six, and in the shopping centers there were a few clusters with as many as fifteen or twenty globes. Blade saw one group of thirteen Menel and twelve Kananites take over one of the large clusters and settle down for a long conference. In fact, the conference went on so long that somebody eventually ordered dinner and a swarm of Menel and robot waiters brought out a dozen carts loaded with food and drink.

"That's the first dinner party I've ever seen where all the conversation has to go through a computerized translator," said Blade. "It might be a good idea to apply back home to fight bores. Somebody gets drunk or tries to monopolize the conversation, you pull the plug, and that's the last of him for the rest of the evening!"

Riyannah laughed. "I've been tempted to do that a few times myself. Some of the Menel take themselves so seriously. The Goran of Scientists are about the worst. But it's considered very bad manners to cut somebody off unless they've actually gone to sleep, turned violet, or started making love.

"The content and structure of the two languages aren't too far apart," Riyannah went on. "In fact they're amazingly close together, considering how physically different we and the Menel are."

"I know what you mean," Blade said. "Our own scien-

94

tists have sometimes argued that two races from different worlds could only understand each other if they were physically alike. Perhaps that's why I found it so easy to learn Targan."

"Perhaps," said Riyannah. They were both silent for a moment, remembering that Blade's similarity to the Targans had already caused some trouble and might cause more.

"In any case, although we think very much alike, we cannot speak alike. We have lungs, tongues, lips, and vocal cords. They have a system of vibrating disks of bone and air tubes that can be shut off or opened. They can't make any of the sounds of our language and we can't make any of the sounds of theirs."

"That must have caused trouble back when you'd just met the Menel."

"It did. Fortunately both sides wanted to solve the problem. They called on their best linguists and their biggest computers. They used sign language and pictures to work out a basic vocabulary. Then they put the vocabulary into the computer and designed Speakers to duplicate the sounds of either language. That was most of the work. We've just been adding to the vocabulary and building bigger computers ever since."

"I see. Kananites and Menel can't talk to each other without the Speakers?"

"No."

A good deal now fell into place for Blade. Kananites and Menel rode as passengers in each other's ships, but the crews were always all-Kananite or all-Menel. A spaceship crew had to have almost instant communication. Even if the ship's computer could run a Speaker, there would be too much of a delay. In combat it would be worse, and if the computer was damaged so that the crew couldn't talk to each other that would be the end of everything.

For the same reason Kananites and Menel each had their own half of the asteroid and kept pretty much to it. They mixed freely only in the central cave, the recreational area common to both races. The asteroid's computers could handle translating five or six hundred Kanan-Menel conversations but not five or six thousand. Kananites and Menel could get along quite well enough even when living and working apart most of the time.

Living and working, yes—but what about fighting? What was going to happen when *Dark Warrior* was finished and Loyun Chard sent her out to attack the asteroid? For the first time Menel and Kananite would be fighting literally side by side. What would happen to the base then, particularly if the computers were damaged and the Speakers started going out?

Blade decided he'd better find out what plans were being made to meet the coming Targan attack. Part of his decision was pure self-interest. He might still be on the asteroid when the attack came and he didn't want to be a helpless bystander.

Most of his decision was a desire to help. He was now certain that Riyannah was telling the truth about the Kananites and the Menel. Both races were better than the Targans as they would be under the rule of Loyun Chard. They deserved all the help he could give them.

Now to find out how much that would be.

Blade did his best to be helpful, but promptly ran into several stone walls. To start with, he wasn't even allowed to visit two-thirds of the asteroid. That two-thirds included practically everything he wanted to see, particularly the asteroid's own defense weapons.

Blade was finally able to get hold of a plan of the asteroid and study it closely. He still hadn't been hooked up to one of the Teacher Globes to have a knowledge of the Kananite language implanted directly in his brain. He was beginning to suspect this wasn't accidental. In spite of this he'd picked up enough Kananite to be able to read the plan fairly well.

After a few hours' study he concluded that the asteroid was unarmed except for the weapons aboard the patrol ships based there. The Menel and the Kananites had spared no expense fitting it out with laboratories, observatories, repair shops, and living quarters with all the comforts of home for both races. They hadn't given it a single heavy weapon.

This seemed so ridiculous to Blade that he asked Riyannah what the real situation was. He was hoping to be told that there were asteroid-based weapons the plan didn't show and that he couldn't be told about.

Instead Riyannah nodded. "You are quite right. Except for the patrol ships, the base has no defenses."

"Why? I can understand why it wasn't armed when the Targans didn't have a space fleet. But now they're building the starship as fast as they can, and she'll be only the first of many. Surely the base ought to have *something*."

Riyannah smiled sadly. "It should. But there's a reason for its being unarmed, a very simple reason. Richard, I don't think you understand just how the Twenty Cities of Kanan deal with each other."

"Apparently I don't." He found it impossible to keep an edge out of his voice, although he knew he ought to. Riyannah wasn't responsible for this situation, and it wasn't fair to take out his irritation on her simply because she was the only Kananite he could talk to.

Riyannah explained. Each of the Twenty Cities of Kanan was completely independent in all the material things of life. This was inevitable when the energy came from the sun and food, clothing, and housing could literally be extracted from the air, the water, and the earth. So there was no need to fight or compete over resources.

On the other hand, there was a continuous struggle, polite but very stubborn, for prestige. A City could win a victory in this struggle by discovering a new planet, developing a new art form, winning an athletic competition, or doing something to impress the Menel.

"What do the Menel think of this game-playing?" Blade asked.

"The Menel are a united planet. Their only divisions are those among the different Gorani. They don't really understand what we're doing. I think they would call it silly, except that they're too polite. In any case they're also realists. They know there's no other way of dealing with Kanan except by allowing the 'game-playing' among the Cities."

"And I should follow the same path as the Menel?" said Blade.

Riyannah shrugged. "You said it, I didn't. But certainly if the Menel haven't been able to change us in five hundred years, you aren't going to do it."

The Twenty Cities of Kanan could cooperate if there was a good reason. There'd been a good reason when it came time to establish the asteroid base for keeping watch on the Targans. Every City contributed people and equipment and resources to setting it up. Everyone recognized the need for the base. They also recognized that contributing generously was one way of showing off before the other Cities and the Menel.

So the base was finished. Every City contributed, but no City wanted to risk another's getting control of the base. It was too valuable. So the Kananites who manned it were carefully chosen in equal proportions from all twenty Cities. The important leadership positions were carefully rotated among people from the distant cities.

Finally, it was absolutely forbidden to arm the base. Each City sent a few armed patrol ships to help defend it, but that was all. No one wanted to risk what might happen if the base was armed. Then one City might suddenly gain control of it and be able to defend it against the ships of the other Cities. That might even lead to war among the Kananites, or at least to some fairly serious fighting.

The base was not that valuable in itself. The resources put into it were small compared to the total wealth of Kanan. It was just that whichever City took it over would win a great prestige victory, making the other Cities look foolish in the eyes of the Menel.

It was a very simple situation, one that could lead to defeat and disaster for the Kananites. They'd abolished war but they hadn't abolished competition, politics, or intrigue. In fact they were so in love with their polite politcal rivalries that they seemed ready to sacrifice lives and wealth rather than give them up.

"Don't the governments of the Twenty Cities realize that the situation is changing fast?" he asked. "If the base can't defend itself, everybody is going to lose. Everybody is going to look silly in front of Menel, and perhaps worse. Do you think the Menel will be happy having their people die because the Kananites want to go on playing games?" He tried to speak calmly and almost succeeded.

"Blade, please," said Riyannah, raising a hand to stroke his cheek. "I am not one of the high leaders even of my own City, let alone one who sits on the Council of Kanan. I am a scientist and your friend. That is all. I cannot even get a word from the Council here on the asteroid, when you will be taught Kananite or sent to Kanan! So do not be angry with me for not changing what I cannot change.

Do you think I want the Targans defeated any less than you do?"

"No, Riyannah. I shouldn't have let myself become angry with you. But damn it, you people can't sit around much longer, never mind who's to blame for what!"

"I'm sure the Kanan Council knows this as well as you do," she said. "Or at least they will, once they receive word of Chard's starship. Certainly they will send more patrol ships here. Anything more will take time. The old way of doing things has kept the peace on Kanan for a thousand years. Do you want us to risk becoming like the Targans in order to defeat them?"

"Of course not."

There wasn't much else to say. The Kananites had certainly accomplished something worthwhile by outlawing war. Unfortunately they'd also outlawed quick decision-making, even when they badly needed it. Loyun Chard didn't sound like the sort of man to wait around politely while his enemies argued over the best way to fight him.

The days dragged on, one by one, slowly adding up to weeks. Blade had given up hope of being taught the Kananite language. All he hoped for now was a starship to Kanan, where he might be allowed to put his case before the Council of Kanan. He was prepared to use Riyannah as an interpreter if necessary.

More days. Blade began to wonder if the asteroid Council had decided he shouldn't go to Kanan at all. What was wrong with them? Did they think he was a Targan in disguise? He knew Riyannah was practically camping on the Council's doorstep, but it didn't seem to be doing any good. Blade began to feel like a caged tiger, and sometimes he couldn't keep himself from snarling at Riyannah.

Then at last the Menel came to his rescue.

Riyannah returned one evening from her daily visit to the Council office with a broad grin on her face and several bottles under her arm.

"We can celebrate, Richard," she said, kissing him. "We're going to Kanan in a Menel ship!"

Blade grinned. "Did you have anything to do with this, by some chance?"

"I suppose I did. There was the commander of the Menel patrol ships at the base. When I talked to him about how his people in the two ships we saw died, I mentioned our own problems. He said he couldn't promise anything, but he'd speak to the other Menel leaders here."

"I thought the Menel might have their own opinions on all this—delay," Blade said. He'd almost said "nonsense," but he didn't want to be rude, not with the first battle won. "When do we leave?"

"The ship will be landing here tomorrow. Then they'll have to unload its cargo and passengers. We'll be on our way in two or three days."

Blade started twisting the top off one of the bottles. "Riyannah, get some glasses. We are indeed going to celebrate." Then he noticed that Riyannah was unfastening her tunic. He smiled.

"All right. There's more than one way to celebrate, and we've got plenty of time."

Chapter 14

The Menel ship had only one cabin fitted out for humanoid passengers, and that was obviously a hasty job. The mattress on the bed was as hard as concrete and humped in the middle so that anyone on it tended to roll off the bed the minute they fell asleep. The rug on the floor seemed to have bits of broken glass embedded in it. The walls were covered with tiles in putrid greens and browns. Blade got the general impression that whoever fitted out the cabin had heard of humanoid beings and perhaps even seen pictures of them, but no more.

Fortunately the Menel breathed the same kind of air and drank the same kind of water as Kananites and humans. With a case of food and another case of wine Blade and Riyannah expected to stay alive, if not exactly comfortable, all the way to Kanan.

On the wall of the cabin just above the bed was a large square of bronze-tinted glass. "That's the ship's entertainment system," said Riyannah. "We can leave it off most of the time, unless you really want to watch discussions of the work of a Menel playwright who's been dead for more than a thousand years. I can even ask the captain to leave it off when we make our Transition."

The Kananites and Menel used a faster-than-light drive that depended on a Zin Field—Pursas Zin being the Kananite scientist who'd discovered it. When the Zin Field reached a critical strength, the ship generating it dropped out of normal space into—somewhere else. For some unguessable time it was nowhere and nowhen in terms of conventional, relativistic space. Then the Transition came to an end and the ship reappeared, four or five light-years from where it had been.

In the early days of interstellar flight, a good many ships turned on their Zin Fields, entered the Transition, and never came out again. Over the centuries both Kananites and Menel refined the process and reduced the risks. Now it was considered cause for alarm if one ship was lost in Transition every ten years out of the thousand or so the Menel and Kananites had shuttling back and forth among the stars.

Blade wanted to see the Transition. "I've been through enough of them in our own ships. I'd like to see how yours compares with ours."

"Wouldn't they be the same, if the principles of the drive are the same?"

Blade shook his head. "I'm not a power plant engineer, remember? I don't even know if your drive engines look like ours, let alone work the same way."

"Very well," said Riyannah. "I thought I'd warn you, because some Transitions are incredibly violent. People have been known to go temporarily insane or be unconscious for several days. At the very least you may get sick to your stomach."

"We'll put a bucket beside the bed," said Blade, laughing. "Blast it, Riyannah, anyone would think you didn't want me to watch the Transition."

He'd said it as a joke, but didn't miss the swift change of expression on her face at the words. She was trying to keep him from watching the Transition, or at least suspected someone else would be happier if he didn't—someone in authority.

He'd have to be careful when the Transition came, hiding any physical reactions as much as he could. Otherwise he might blow his cover story of being an experienced space traveller. Riyannah might become suspicious, and then—well, she'd never let her affection for him drive her to putting her people in danger. He was sure of that.

Even if she didn't become suspicious herself, once more there was the possibility of her saying the wrong thing to the wrong person. If the Kananites played politics the way Riyannah described, many of them would be shrewd, skeptical observers, with a keen eye for flaws in a cover story.

Damn it, though, what did he have to worry about? His brain and body had survived all the numerous transitions from Dimension to Dimension. Surely they wouldn't let him down over a leap across a mere few light-years?

Besides, he was going to be the first man of Home Dimension Earth ever to travel across interstellar space. He wanted to be awake, aware, and watching when the moment came.

Blade and Riyannah went aboard the ship, unpacked their gear, and ate dinner. Two hours later the ship took off. On the screen Blade saw the asteroid shrink slowly. On the half turned toward the sun, light blazed from the polished metal of the buildings on the surface. On the half in shadow, chains of multicolored lights looped and spiraled everywhere. It looked magnificent, and also horribly vulnerable.

The asteroid shrank until it was no more than the brightest of a thousand stars on the screen. Then suddenly the stars turned into ragged globes of light, spreading out until they met and mingled. They were visibly crawling across the screen, and at the same time Blade felt the floor under him vibrating like a giant's drum. Then the screen went blank.

Blade lay back among the pillows and tried to brace himself in a position where he wouldn't roll off the bed. The ship was accelerating now at nearly a quarter the speed of light, racing straight away from Targa's sun. It would travel at this speed until it was about five billion miles from the sun. Any closer and the sun's gravity would distort the Zin Field, endangering the ship.

A quarter of the speed of light. Fast enough to travel from the Earth to the Moon in six seconds. Nothing sent out into space by Home Dimension Earth had ever reached more than a tiny fraction of that speed. Some scientists in Home Dimension said nothing ever could reach it. Yet the Menel ship, a hundred thousand tons of metal, reached that speed as easily as a car accelerating on a freeway.

The ship was on the Menel "day" of about twenty-nine Home Dimension hours. On the morning of the fourth day, Blade woke up to hear a faint chime going *ting-ting-ting*, not loudly but urgently. The screen was alive with dancing spirals of crimson and green light.

Blade untangled himself from Riyannah and sat up. That woke her. She looked at the screen, then gripped Blade's hand. "That's the Transition warning. If we're go-

103

ing to take any drugs we'd better do it now, to give them time to work." Blade shook his head. "Very well. What about the screen?" Another shake of the head. Riyannah threw her arms wide in a gesture of comic despair. "All right. Don't say afterward I didn't warn you!"

Blade pulled one of the chairs to where he could see the screen without moving his head. Then he sat down in it and leaned back as far as it would let him. Riyannah lay down on the bed, pulled a blanket over her, and braced herself in place with pillows.

The gong sounded again, the same *ting-ting-ting* but now much louder, more like a fire alarm. The spirals on the screen froze, then vanished, leaving the screen glowering darkly down at the cabin.

Then the cabin seemed to burst apart in a sudden, utterly silent explosion. Ceiling, tiled walls, carpeted floor, Riyannah on the bed, the screen itself all rushed away from Blade and vanished into a starless space far too black to be natural. Blade was alone in a void where his eyes saw nothing and the only sound was like a distant organ playing inside his head.

He tried to turn his head and could not. He tried to move his limbs and felt them held rigidly, as if space itself was throwing iron bands around all his joints and muscles. He opened his mouth and tried to shout, but his throat and chest were paralyzed.

Then the organ music in his head swelled, and its pitch rose until it was a torturing scream like a jet engine running up. He felt a shuddering and a vibration all over him, increasing until he knew his bones were pulling apart and his flesh was going to pull free of the bones in another moment.

He was flying apart, and the space around him went red with the agony in his disintegrating body. Then the redness faded, the blackness returned for a moment, and after that he could not even feel whether he was alive or dead.

Blade came back to consciousness lying on his stomach on the floor while Riyannah straddled his buttocks, gently massaging his neck and shoulders. He tried to move and discovered why she was massaging him. Every muscle and joint in his body ached as if he'd been pounded with clubs

104

or crippled by arthritis. He decided to lie quietly and let Riyannah finish her work.

Her slim fingers were strong and highly skilled. After a few minutes Blade felt most of the actual pains fading to dull aches. "All right, Riyannah. Enough." She climbed off him and sat cross-legged on the rug as he rose and tested each arm and leg separately.

"You were unconscious long enough to make me start to worry," she said. "I didn't know if it was your mind or your body, but I was frightened. Menel ships don't carry doctors to treat other races."

Blade found that he was horribly thirsty. He went over to the water tap and drank until all the dryness was out of his throat. Then he took Riyannah in his arms and stroked her hair. He could feel her trembling as he held her.

"This Transition wasn't as long as the ones aboard Earth ships, but it was more intense. Different wavelengths of the two fields, I suppose, but there wasn't anything in it that's going to be dangerous. You don't need to worry about me."

"That's good," said Riyannah slowly. "I—I thought I might have hurt or killed you by getting you aboard a Menel ship. I don't want to think about—"

"So don't think about it," said Blade, silencing her with a kiss. "I needed to get to Kanan, and it was certainly too far to walk."

She laughed, then her hands began moving on him, not massaging but in a different, very familiar way. He picked her up and carried her to the bed, and as he did his lips traveled down her throat to her breasts.

Afterward Riyannah fell asleep as if she'd been stunned. Blade found that once again his mind was working so fast he couldn't have slept if he'd wanted to.

He'd been wired into Lord Leighton's computer and hurled into Dimension X twenty-nine times now. Each time most of the sights and sensations which came to him as his brain twisted were unique. Some of them were identical ones by now, especially the feeling that the fabric of space itself was shaking, tearing, pulling apart, and his own body doing the same. Sometimes that sensation lasted for no more than a few heartbeats, but it was always there, unmistakable and unforgettable.

105

Now he'd felt the exact same sensation as the Menel ship made its Transition across the light-years. Like the geography of Targa, it was hard to believe this was a coincidence. Never mind that the Transition needed a Zin Field generator and the passage between Dimensions used Lord Leighton's computer linked to Blade's mind. There was something the two had in common.

What? Blade realized that the one little word was perhaps the most important question he'd ever faced in the whole history of Project Dimension X. It was also the one he was least likely to have answered.

Did the shift into Dimension X involve a shift in space as well? Blade had often wondered. Did the Transition through space also involve at least a brief passage through another Dimension? Or was it something else entirely, perhaps simpler, perhaps more complicated, certainly beyond Blade's ability to even guess?

Lord Leighton's computer might not be just a flawed, narrow, irregularly open door to other Dimensions. It could become a door to interstellar space, the settlement of other worlds, contact with other intelligent races, the immortality of humanity as it spread out from Earth—

Blade found himself sweating and stopped letting his mind run so far and so fast ahead of the facts. The questions his experiences here raised were nothing less than awesome. He still couldn't hope to answer any of them without the cooperation of the Kananites, and he wasn't even on Kanan yet. Even after he reached the planet, he suspected that getting Kananite cooperation would be a chancy business. And if all the people who could help him were scientists, whose basic language was some completely alien system of mathematics—

Blade realized that for once he was faced with problems which might simply be more than his mind could grasp. For all his gifts he was a practical man of action, not a theoretical scientist. If Lord Leighton were here, he could undoubtedly draw far more conclusions from the same amount of data than Blade could ever hope to. He'd also probably have less trouble getting more information out of the Kananites. Lord Leighton had been hammering appropriations out of boards and committees for nearly fifty years. He could take the Council of Kanan in his stride!

106

Except that Lord Leighton was now not only Dimensions but light-years away. Blade would have to do the best he could with what he knew and hope that would be enough.

Chapter 15

The starship made four more Transitions on its way to Kanan. Blade got used to the effects so quickly that on the last two he didn't even lose consciousness. He still felt the old familiar sensation of wrenched, disrupted space, and talking with Riyannah revealed she felt something very similar. He wasn't particularly surprised, since the Kananites were so humanoid. He wondered what the Menel felt in the moment of a Transition.

In ship's time it took nearly three weeks to complete all five Transitions. They came out of the last Transition on the edge of Kanan's system, thirty light-years from Targa. Then at a leisurely forty-five thousand miles a second they cruised in toward Kanan.

The trip took seven days. Kanan's star was a yellow type G, like Targa's star and like the Sun itself, but rather more massive. So its gravity field was stronger and a starship needed to make its last Transition farther out. Blade found himself growing impatient to reach Kanan, whatever waited for him there, and bored with life aboard ship.

They came into orbit around Kanan from the planet's night side. On the screen Blade saw an immense shadowy globe hanging against the darkness of space. The bluish light of its two moons left shimmering paths on the oceans, but the land masses were black pits.

In each of those pits glowed huge jewels, with a hundred faces in as many different colors—the Cities of Kanan, each holding forty or fifty million people. Around each of them spread a faint dusting of glowing powder—the lights of farms and country retreats. Other dots of light moved swiftly across the face of the darkness—spaceships and space stations in low orbits around the planet.

It was breathtaking, and Riyannah nearly had to drag

Blade away from the screen to start packing their bags for landing. He moved about the cabin with only half his mind on the job. The other half was turning over memories of that jewel-studded globe.

For the first time in weeks, Blade felt strongly the knowledge that he was only one man facing a whole planet which might not be friendly or even cooperative. He also felt something else, just as strong and far less pleasant.

What a magnificent target Kanan made, seen from space!

Blade and Riyannah rode down to the planet's surface aboard an arrow-slim shuttle not much larger than a Home Dimension jet fighter. The shuttle flight took them halfway around the planet and gave Blade a good view of its geography. It had two large continental masses, both in the northern hemisphere, and an Australia sized island occupying most of the north polar region. From the southern end of the larger continent a string of islands trailed off across four thousand miles of ocean. Some of those islands were larger than Britain. Kanan seemed to have a little more water than Earth, but not enough more to crowd the billion Kananites.

Blade also counted at least a dozen large starships in orbit around Kanan, half of them Menel. If he'd still been inclined to distrust the Menel, he would have changed his mind now. One Menel ship with half a dozen hydrogen bombs aboard could slaughter fifty million Kananites in a surprise attack. Yet the Kananites let Menel ships orbit the planet as if they were totally harmless. The Kananites were willing to trust the Menel with the safety of their home planet, and they'd had five hundred years of experience with the walking asparagus stalks. The Kananites might be slow to react to a crisis, but they weren't fools. The Menel were safe.

The shuttle landed on top of a cylindrical building a mile high and three blocks thick, completely covered with shimmering glass. Blade recognized the giant solar collectors which supplied most of the daily energy needs of Kanan. Power cells in the basement kept the building going when the sun wasn't shining and basins on the roof caught and purified rainwater.

Not that the rainwater on Kanan would need much purification, Blade realized. His first few breaths of Kanan's air told him something he should have expected. Kanan's air was completely unpolluted, as clean and sweet as if the planet had never supported a single factory. Blade found it hard to get used to breathing such air with the gleaming buildings of a super-civilization towering in every direction.

The building where they landed was near the center of Mestar, Riyannah's home city. The top half held apartments and a few shops and stores to serve their residents. The lower half housed the laboratories and offices of Mestar's university. Since Riyannah was a teacher at the university, this building was the ideal place for her. All the "commuting" she had to do was climb into an elevator in the central core of the building, drop three thousand feet, then walk a block to her office.

"About half the Kananites who work at all live in the same building as their workplace," she said. "Others work at home, linked to their fellow workers by screens and computer circuits."

That explained another part of Kanan's prosperity. They didn't need to use up energy and other resources moving people from their homes to their work and back again. This had the disadvantage that Kananites spent a large part of their lives in a protected environment, and perhaps explained why they needed "tame" wilderness even when they got outdoors.

After the first weeks in Mestar Blade wasn't sure that anyone except Riyannah in the whole city or on the whole planet knew of his existence. This bothered him. After all, he did represent a whole new race of intelligent space-traveling beings. How could the Kananites take his appearance so casually? If they'd all been furiously at work preparing to face the Targan menace, ignoring him this way would have made sense. Unfortunately Blade saw nothing like that sort of work, although he saw a good deal of Kanan.

Riyannah seemed to have nothing to do except play hostess, guide, and sometimes translator. They traveled all over Mestar on foot, on bicycles, on powered roller skates, in three-wheeled electric cars, and on the high-speed monorails linking all the clusters of buildings.

For longer trips to other cities, the seashore, and the wilderness, they used Riyannah's flyer. It resembled a huge egg, with a transparent large end facing forward and the tail sprouting a large propeller. An antigravity generator kept the flyer in the air while the propeller drove it forward. Both ran off power cells under the cabin floor. The flyer was no faster than a Home Dimension helicopter, but it could fly several hundred miles and land as gently as a soap bubble deep in the wilderness.

The controls of the flyer were so simple that a child could have operated it. After the second week Riyannah taught Blade but never let him take the flyer out alone. She seemed embarrassed at having to refuse, so Blade was careful never to ask her why. He didn't really have to know right now and his distrust would hurt her unnecessarily.

The seats of the flyer were soft and could be folded down to make a bed. Sometimes they would set the automatic pilot, fold down the seats, and make love as the flyer purred along ten thousand feet up. Other times they would fly deep into the wilderness, unpack sleeping gear and food, then spend the night in the open air.

This surprised hiking Kananites who stumbled across their camp. Riyannah answered their questions by explaining that camping was a medical treatment for Blade. As far as Blade could tell, the Kananites seemed to accept her explanation.

By now Blade had taught himself a fair amount of spoken Kananite. He could follow many conversations well enough to have some idea of what they were about, and he could handle much of the business of daily living. He was also careful to leave Riyannah with the impression that he didn't understand a single word of her language. He was quite sure by now that his not being taught Kananite was part of a plan by somebody in power, somebody who could command Riyannah's cooperation in the plan. He was supposed to stay cut off from the rest of Kanan until the powers that be found it convenient to change the situation. Blade didn't particularly like this, but he was willing to live with it. Proving how much Kananite he knew would do little good. It would simply embarrass Riyannah and possibly provoke a crisis with her superiors.

After two more weeks, Blade began to wonder if he

111

ought to provoke that crisis, no matter how much it embarrassed Riyannah! The Kananites were too civilized to execute him, no matter how much uproar he made. They were also too civilized to do anything at all unless he kicked them as hard as he could in the shins!

Blade didn't entirely blame them. They had a real Utopia on Kanan, with cheap and abundant energy, no pollution, every luxury one could ask for, education and travel available to all, universal good health and three-hundred year lifespans. It was a magnificent civilization, and under other circumstances Blade wouldn't have dreamed of doing anything against it. In fact he suspected he would have been quite happy to settle down with Riyannah and spend the rest of his life on Kanan.

Unfortunately he had his duties to Project Dimension X, which meant returning to Targa as soon as possible. He wasn't going to gamble on Lord Leighton's computer being able to reach across thirty light-years of space as well as across the Dimensions. He'd learned far too much that he had to bring home if he could.

He also had his duty to Kanan. He owed them all the help he could give them against the Targans, help they might badly need. He couldn't do very much as long as they expected him to stay deaf and dumb.

Yet they would go on expecting him to do just that, unless he gave them some good reason to do otherwise. Blade thought he now knew the Kananites' basic weakness. With their prosperity, their peace, and their long lives, they'd become afraid to take risks. They could still compete, as the gentle rivalry of the Cities proved, but only within narrow limits. Outside those narrow limits, all the Kananites saw was the risk of losing something they valued. Yet Loyun Chard and the Targans were going to have to be met outside those safe, comfortable limits.

Blade started considering ways of pushing the Kananites into doing some hard thinking. Fortunately it wouldn't be quite as bloody a process as the war with the Targans. He'd need a weapon and a flyer, though, and it would be a good idea if Riyannah could be persuaded to stand clear. Accidents could happen, and even Kananites might get angry enough to shoot.

There were a lot of details to be worked out. It took several days, and he had to deceive Riyannah every waking minute of those days. There were times when Blade wondered if it was worth the trouble.

Then a week later they took Blade down to the university and put him under a Teacher Globe. It turned out his planning hadn't been wasted after all.

Chapter 16

Blade awoke with a pounding headache, a dry mouth, and several spots on his skin that itched uncomfortably. He awoke slowly, his thoughts sluggish and his senses blunted, but he still realized the moment he opened his eyes that he wasn't in his own room in Riyannah's apartment. This one had pale white walls, a dark green floor covering, no furniture except a bedside table, and no artwork on the walls or any place else. It looked rather like a hospital room, and Blade wondered if something had gone wrong with his language instruction.

Trying to think seemed to make his headache worse. He relaxed and tried to breathe slowly and steadily. Gradually the headache faded. Now he could see a pitcher of water and a glass on the bedside table. He drank until he had the strength to sit up and look around more carefully.

The room still looked depressingly plain. The itching spots on his skin turned out to be several minor burns, covered with a grayish ointment. There was one on each thigh, another on his right temple, and two more close together at the base of his spine. He was wearing heavy gray pajamas.

Blade climbed out of bed and paced out the dimensions of the room. It was about twenty feet on a side and all the walls were padded with something like coarse fur. As he approached the center of the wall opposite the bed, a section of it slid open. Blade passed through the doorway and down three steps into a sunken room the same size as the bedroom. This room had pale red walls and a blue floor, both well padded. It was furnished with a long couch, a padded bench, and two chairs apparently built up out of threads of spun plastic. All the furniture was fastened immovably to the floor.

Was this a hospital, or had the Kananites somehow got

114

the idea he was dangerous or insane? The padded walls and furniture reminded Blade unpleasantly of the padded cells of Home Dimension asylums.

On one side of the living room was a grayish patch the height of a man. Blade walked over to it. As he approached the gray patch it folded itself upward. Behind it was a glowing metal box, with several dials, two faucets, a large slot, and several knobs.

Blade stepped up to the box, and suddenly the dials *made sense!* One of them was a temperature gauge, another a clock, a third showed pressure. A piece of plastic with printing on it lay in the slot. Blade picked it up and the printed words seemed to jump off the plastic into his brain. The metal box was a food-processing machine, and here were detailed instructions for its use.

Blade's sigh of relief nearly blew the plastic sheet across the room. Whatever else might have happened, he'd learned Kananite. He retrieved the plastic sheet and tried reading the instructions out loud. His vocal cords, tongue, and lips combined to produced the clipped, high-pitched words of the Kananite language.

It was an impressive achievement, implanting the whole language in his brain this way. The secret of the Teacher Globes would be something worth having. It would be an enormous blessing to a Home Dimension where education fought a desperate battle with rapidly-accumulating facts. It might even help Lord Leighton understand what happened to Blade's brain as he passed into Dimension X so that he could speak the local language. For the moment the most important thing was that Blade could talk freely with his hosts or captors. He wasn't sure which they were now, but at least he had some chance of finding out.

Blade made another test of his new knowledge by dialing for a menu, then ordering a meal. It came out hot and steaming, spiced exactly as he'd ordered it, complete with a bottle of wine. Blade found he was both hungry and thirsty and made a hearty meal. He obviously wasn't going to starve to death, even if he had to stay here until the Kananites made up their minds about him.

Unfortunately good food wouldn't make any difference if the Kananites took as long to reach that decision as he expected. He could sit here in comfort for months or years, knowing nothing of the outside world, nothing

115

about Riyannah, nothing about the crisis with Targa, cut off from Lord Leighton's computer by the light-years between Targa and Kanan. He might sit here until the outside world finally penetrated in the form of a Targan H-bomb bursting over Mestar.

Blade finished his meal, put the dishes and bottle in the food machine's slot, and watched them vanish. Then he began to explore the living room, searching for other machines or a door.

He found the second door the same way he'd found the first. Something in it sensed his presence and it quietly slid open. Blade looked out into a surprisingly normal Kananite hallway. The floor was pebbled metal with inlays of pastel mosaics. The walls were plain white, but carvings of veined bluish wood hung from golden brackets every few yards. With almost universal leisure, two-thirds of Kanan's people had at least one artistic hobby. Original paintings and sculptures were displayed in the local equivalent of hot dog stands and car washes.

Blade stepped through the door and walked toward the bend in the hall about fifty feet away. He'd covered half the distance when a man and a woman came around the bend. Like most Kananites indoors, they were lightly dressed. The woman wore a short sleeveless dress, belted with a green sash, and was barefoot. The man wore a similar sash holding up bell-bottomed trousers. His chest was bare and painted in swirling abstract designs of green and purple. Both were also carrying pistol-sized hurd-rays in shoulder holsters. They were the first armed people Blade had seen on Kanan, and they confirmed his suspicions. Whether he was a guest or a prisoner, he was certainly under restraint now.

Blade smiled politely as the two guards approached. He noted that both of them came within easy striking range before stopping, instead of one standing back to cover the other.

"I'm sorry to bother you," he said in perfect Kananite. "But the food machine gave off some smoke when it took the dishes and bottles after the meal. Should it do this?"

The woman shook her head. "No. We'll have the system checked out and send maintenance people if necessary. Is there anything else?"

"Not today, thank you."

"Good." The woman gave a pasted-on smile that didn't reach her eyes. "Have a good night's sleep." The note of polite dismissal in her voice was unmistakable and Blade took the hint. The last thing he wanted to do at the moment was make the people guarding him suspicious.

Blade found a bathroom on the far side of the bedroom. He took a leisurely shower, and as he soaped himself he mentally revised his plans. He was still going to have to do something drastic to make the Kananites notice him. Obviously they had ideas about him they hadn't had before. Perhaps they'd probed his mind and revealed his true background and history, including the existence of Dimension X. That meant his situation could be acutely dangerous now, but there was nothing he could do about it—except act as quickly as possible.

Dimension X or no Dimension X, he'd have to get out of here or at least make a damned good try at it! If he got out, he'd find ways of making the Kananites know they had someone unusual on their hands, who couldn't be ignored while they played politics-as-usual. Even if he didn't get all the way out, even making the effort might send the same message.

In some ways he was worse off than he'd been. He didn't know where he was, he was watched and guarded, and there wasn't anything in his quarters to use as a weapon. On the other hand, the guards didn't look very alert. If he could surprise them he could certainly handle them with his bare hands. Then he'd have their guns and a clear road at least to the end of the hall. Finally, Riyannah was nowhere around. There wouldn't be any danger of her getting hit by a stray shot if it came to shooting. There wasn't even much danger of her being held responsible for his escape and anything that came of it. He hoped she'd realize that his motives were honest, although he doubted she'd be in a position to help him even if she wanted to.

Chapter 17

Blade tested the skill and alertness of his guards three more times in the next two days. After that he decided to make his move for real the next time. Any more tests and the guards might become suspicious enough to call for more reinforcements than he could handle.

The clock was striking the fifteenth period of Kanan's twenty-period day. Outside it would be nearly dark. He'd have the cover of night for the first stage of his travels, and that could make a difference. The Kananites certainly had the technology to track down fugitives and criminals but they had very little crime. The human skills for using the equipment might be more than a little rusty.

The food machines would produce anything Blade wanted. He dialed for three loaves of bread, a slab of cheese, and a two-foot length of sausage. When they appeared he popped them into a pillowcase, added two pairs of socks and a spare shirt from the wardrobe in the bedroom, then tied everything into a bundle. He stepped up to the living room wall, the door opened, and he was out in the hallway.

Ten steps, and a solitary guard appeared around the bend. Blade hurled his bundle with all the strength in his right arm, striking the guard in the face before he could take another step. Blade closed, twisted the hurd-ray out of the man's hand as he drew, and punched him in the jaw. Kananite men were almost as slender as the women and Blade had to pull the punch not to knock the man's head off his shoulders. The guard flew across the hallway, thudded into the wall, and slumped limply to the floor.

Blade retrieved his bundle and raised the pistol just as the second guard hurried around the bend. She trotted right into the hurd-ray from Blade's pistol, set low to stun rather than kill. Her own pistol skidded across the floor in one direction while her unconscious body skidded in another. Blade scooped up the fallen pistol without missing a step, then broke into a run.

Beyond the bend Blade found a small room, furnished with a sofa, a couple of chairs, and a small green console. A gray-haired woman sat at the console, watching the display of lights. On the sofa a young man was sound asleep.

Blade came around the bend as the woman rose from her chair and said sharply:

"Durnann, wake up! Something's—" She broke off as she saw Blade, then started to draw her gun. Blade stunned her and she collapsed on top of the young man. He woke up, saw Blade, and stared.

"Which way out?" said Blade.

The man's mouth opened as wide as his eyes, then he got himself under control enough to point to a shallow archway on the right. Blade put one pistol on a high setting and blew up the green console. Smoke swirled as he walked over to the archway and a door opened in front of him. Outside was darkness, cool night air, and a landing platform with a small dark blue flyer parked near the edge. Blade felt like cheering.

"Thank you," he said to the young man, who still lay rigid on the couch, the woman on top of him. Blade stepped through the door and it slid shut behind him. He fused one edge of it with the hurd-ray to make sure it would stay shut. With no communications and no door, the people inside would have a little trouble spreading the word of his escape.

Then he hurried to the flyer. It was the same model that Riyannah had taught him to fly, and the gauges showed the power cells were fully charged. Behind the pack seat he found a box of hiking gear, including two canteens and some packages of concentrated food. He also found a hurd-ray rifle with a computerized laser sight and half a dozen extra power cells, obviously a military or police weapon. His luck seemed to be getting better and better.

He tossed his pillowcase full of food and spare clothing on top of the other gear, then sat down. He cut in the power, adjusted the anti-gravity, and started the propeller. The little machine shot off the landing platform and out into the night. Blade climbed until he could see the ranked towers of Mestar spread out below him, marching away into the night. Each tower blazed with lights in gold and green, purple and red, silver and blue, some dancing and twinkling, others shining steadily like the stars overhead. Blade turned the nose of the flyer toward where the ranks of towers faded away into the darkness of the wilderness. Then he increased the power and the whine of the propeller swelled.

The power cells couldn't last very long at this rate, but Blade didn't need the flyer very long either. An hour later and a hundred and fifty miles from his starting place, he buzzed a summer cabin by a small lake. Firing the rifle through the flyer's open window he knocked the top off the cabin's chimney. Lights were just coming on inside as Blade sped off a few feet above the treetops.

Now a clearing opened below him. He landed, set the automatic pilot, and dropped to the ground with all his gear as the flyer began to rise again. It rose above the treetops, then went humming off back toward the cabin. It had another half hour's power in its cells and with luck any pursuers would chase it, not him, for at least that long.

Blade wondered when those pursuers would be showing up. Sooner or later someone would notice he was missing and take whatever the Kananites considered drastic action. He wondered what that would be and how long it would take them to catch him.

He hoped it would be quite a while. He'd made a good start with his escape, but nothing more. He'd have to stay on the loose and do a good deal more before it became completely impossible for the Kananites to ignore him.

The flyer was out of sight now. Blade slung his rifle and headed into the forest. *This is where I came in,* he thought. *Alone in the forest, on a strange world.*

Blade's escape from Mestar did everything he'd hoped it would and a good deal more besides. He not only got the government of Kanan moving, he got himself into Kanan's history books for the next century.

He even had his adventures made into a popular comedy, *Blade in the Forest.* One of the planet's leading playwrights wrote it, and it was performed at least once a year for the next fifty years.

It was not performed in Mestar, though. When it was

performed in other cities, it was always possible to tell who in the audience came from Mestar. They were the ones who weren't laughing. Blade succeeded in his plan, and also in making Mestar and its people look like bungling idiots. They managed to forgive him, but they were never able to forget the affair enough to laugh at themselves over it.

Blade roamed through the farms, the resorts, and the wilderness around Mestar for eleven days. He left behind him a trail of irritating minor damage and of thoroughly embarrassed Mestarians. Except for the people he'd knocked out making his escape not one man, woman, or child picked up so much as a bruise from Blade's work. On the other hand, none of the people who ran into him found him easy to forget.

There was the time he came on a party of six people holding a quiet little orgy in a secluded forest clearing. From two hundred yards away he carefully burned all their clothes to ashes with the rifle. Then he vanished like the smoke from the fires, leaving the six people to climb into their flyers and head for home stark naked.

There was the time he climbed to the roof of a cottage equipped with an old-fashioned woodburning fireplace and blocked the chimney. Smoke promptly started rolling out the doors and windows, followed by half a dozen furiously coughing Kananites.

There was the time he slipped on to a farm where they raised riding animals, opened the barn door, and let all the stock out. The freed animals scattered in all directions and fell on the neighbors' vegetable gardens like a plague of locusts. The farmer had to retrieve all of his stock and face the indignation of his neighbors as well.

There was the time he slipped into a deserted wilderness camp and went to work. He knocked down the approach bridge and dropped all the bedding from the cabins into the nearest stream. Then he went to the bathrooms, set the showers to produce nothing but cold water, and adjusted the toilets to back up violently if anyone tried to flush them.

After the first three days Blade had to be a little more careful. From the number of flyers he saw in the sky it seemed likely the Mestarians were finally coming after him. Now it was time to lead his pursuers on the longest and merriest chase possible.

Blade managed to stretch that chase out for a week. It wasn't always easy, because his pursuers were numerous even if unskilled. He found he had to avoid moving by day, and was never able to sleep for more than a couple of hours at a time. His shoes wore through and he had to move on barefooted. His clothes became ragged, but he didn't dare try to capture new ones even if he could have found a Kananite whose clothes would have fit him. He ran out of emergency rations and could no longer risk approaching any campground or cabin to steal food. They were all guarded now. So he went back to eating berries and mushrooms and raw fish. He grew gaunt and grim-looking, his skin dark with sun and dirt, his beard and hair bristling in all directions.

He'd seldom had more fun in his entire life.

Eventually Blade decided that the time for fun was over. He must have a small army chasing him now, and among them were bound to be one or two hotheads who might be getting a little trigger-happy. It was time to let himself be captured and move on to the next stage of his plan.

So on the morning of the eleventh day he woke up, caught two fish, built a fire, and settled down to let his breakfast cook and his pursuers see the smoke. In less than an hour two flyers swooped low overhead, heads sticking out of their side windows. One of the flyers dashed off to the west, no doubt to call up reinforcements. The other started circling the clearing, staying carefully outside the lethal range of Blade's rifle.

Minutes passed, turning into an hour, then two. Blade began to wonder who they were calling up by way of reinforcements. The circling flyer was replaced by two new ones. Blade finished the last of the fish and began to dig a small pit for the bones and guts.

Then a shadow passed over the clearing. Blade looked up and saw a full-sized spaceship hanging in the sky over the treetops. It was at least two hundred feet long, and the half-dozen flyers holding formation on either side of it looked like pilotfish escorting a shark. Behind the first ship came a second, even larger. Blade recognized the second one as a Menel ship.

Blade backed slowly toward the trees, holding his rifle ready to fire. This was really calling up the reinforcements! Those two ships could be carrying enough firepower to blast half the forest. He wasn't sure why things were being done this way, and he also didn't want to be a sitting target in the open while he found out.

He'd just reached the trees when an enormously amplified voice boomed down from the first ship:

"Blade—come out and join us. We will listen to whatever you have to say. Come out now and nothing will happen to you."

Blade shouted as loud as he could, hoping he'd be heard. "Who is the 'we'? What I have to say is for the Council of Kanan. Are you Council members?"

"No, but—"

Good. They could hear him. "I've been kept waiting too long already. You've been wasting time and giving it to the Targans. I won't help you waste any more time playing games. It's your world, not—"

A new voice cut in. In spite of distortion from the amplification, Blade recognized Riyannah, tense and desperate. "Blade, you'll get to the Council of Kanan. If these fools won't—"

"Shut up, you filthy traitor whore! You've already done—" the voice broke off in sounds of scuffling. A man's voice was cursing incoherently, then Riyannah screamed in unmistakable pain.

Blade hit the ground, raising his rifle and sighting on the nearest flyer as he did. "If any of you bastards lays one more finger on Riyannah, I'll start shooting."

The man's voice was trembling with rage. "You can't hope to win, Blade. Come out now and—"

"Be burned down? What kind of a fool do you think—?" He broke off as he saw one of the flyers turn and start to drop toward the clearing.

Suddenly crimson flamed from the bow of the Menel ship. It was only a low-powered blast, but precisely aimed. Air crackled and the flyer's propeller became a puff of greasy smoke. Still supported by its anti-gravity, the machine bobbed helplessly, like a cork in a boiling pot. Then a new voice broke in.

"Richard Blade, far traveler, who would be a friend. We will let no harm come to you. We have sworn this,

123

and we do not break our oaths. Come out, and come under our protection if you do not trust those of Kanan."

Blade recognized the voice of a Menel coming through a Speaker. So that was why the reinforcements had come in two spaceships. They needed something big enough to carry Speakers and the computers for them. But why the Menel at all, and why this promise to him? Most important, could he trust it?

Certainly it was hard to trust the man who seemed to command the Kananites. He'd called Riyannah a traitor, struck her, been ready to order his flyers to open fire on Blade. Why Blade wasn't sure, but he'd be dead if the Menel hadn't intervened. Whether or not the Menel had sworn on oath to protect him, they'd been willing to do so—willing enough to shoot at Kananites! If he was that important to the Menel, perhaps he could trust them.

"All right," he shouted. "I'll come out, on two conditions. First, you set Riyannah down on the ground, *now*!

"Second, we both go wherever we're going in the Menel ship. Any Kananite who gets within rifle range of me in the next hour is going to get a hurd-ray through his guts."

The silence following Blade's conditions lasted so long he began to wonder if they'd ever heard him. Then a hatch slid open in the belly of the Kananite ship. A slim figure dropped through the opening, held by a sling on the end of a wire. Blade slung his rifle and sprinted across the clearing in time to help Riyannah out of the sling. She was shaking all over, and would have fallen to the ground if he hadn't told her.

After a moment she got herself under control and managed a feeble smile. Blade noticed that one eye was swollen half-shut.

"Did that bastard—?"

"He did, but don't worry about him. He was acting without orders, and when they hear what he did and what the Menel did after that—" Her smile was grim. "I suspect he'd prefer having you beat him to what's going to happen to him."

"What—?"

"I'll tell you once we're out of here. That, and many other things." Looking over Riyannah's shoulder Blade saw a flyer dropping from the Menel ship and heading toward them.

"All right." He suspected what some of these things might be and knew that others would be complete surprises. None of them would be as big a surprise as the situation he was in now.

He'd fought the Menel twice, in two Dimensions. Now he owed his life and much of his hope of success to their protection.

If anyone had ever told me I'd be trusting my life to the Menel, I'd have rung for the doctor and had them taken away.

Then the flyer was landing and the pilot was sticking his head out the window, urgently waving all four arms and clicking his claws.

Chapter 18

The Menel spaceship went into orbit around Kanan and stayed there for several hours. Riyannah had plenty of time to tell Blade what led up to the confontation over the clearing. She answered most of his questions and he didn't want to bother her with the rest. She looked as if she hadn't had a good meal or a full night's sleep in nearly a month.

As Blade suspected, they'd done more than teach him the Kananite language while they had him under the Teacher Globe. They'd explored his memories from top to bottom and learned the truth about where he came from and how he'd come to Targa.

"I didn't feel happy about how you'd lied to me," said Riyannah. "But I could see that you had many reasons for doing so. Everyone was particularly interested in your two meetings with the Menel."

"I can imagine," said Blade.

"I don't think you can," said Riyannah. "They may have been the most important things you ever did." After listening to her for a while longer, Blade began to suspect she was right. He'd known it was only common sense and basic decency to avoid killing Menel unnecessarily. He couldn't have guessed how much would eventually depend on that common sense and basic decency.

The first person to get involved in the situation after Blade's examination was Vruomanh, Second Councilor of Mestar, a gifted scientist but also an ambitious and intolerant man. He had the notion of keeping Blade under guard while methods were developed for exploring his brain more deeply. Such methods might kill him, but that wouldn't matter. When they'd finished exploring his brain, Mestar would have the Dimension X secret. Then they could use it to win the war against Targa single-handed.

All the other Cities would be eternally grateful to Mestar, which would then become virtually the ruler of Kanan.

"I imagine that idea wasn't entirely unpopular among the Councilors of Mestar," said Blade drily.

"No, it wasn't. But there were a few Councilors who opposed it. My uncle Yu Hardannah was one. There were others who thought it might be a good idea, but needed more study first. Vruomanh didn't like the thought of waiting. He pointed out that if we delayed, the secret might get out and Mestar would lose its chance."

"He was right, wasn't he?"

"He certainly was. I made sure the secret got out. I went straight to the Menel Degdar—I think your word is 'ambassador'—and told him everything. Meanwhile my uncle was making sure they didn't put a Trail Voice in your head, and—"

"A Trail Voice?"

"Yes. It's a little radio transmitter they can put in a person's skull. After that they can pick up the transmissions and know exactly where he is."

"I see." Blade also saw what a narrow escape he'd had. With a radio beacon blatting away in his skull, he'd have been picked up within hours after his escape. As it was—

"They didn't have any method of tracking me without the Trail Voice, did they?"

"No. You're the first fugitive they've had to track without one in something like two hundred years."

No wonder the Targans were a trifle out of practice chasing escaped criminals. "I owe your uncle a great deal."

"Yes. He pointed out that your brain was something unknown. Putting a Trail Voice in your head might destroy your ability to travel among the Dimensions."

Another narrow escape. Riyannah's uncle might very well be right. Being stuck here on Kanan as a friend or ally would be bad enough. Being stuck here as a pawn in some ambitious politician's schemes was something Blade was very glad not to be facing.

Not knowing any of this, Blade escaped. His escape promptly made an already confused and complicated situation even worse. As a Councilor, Riyannah's uncle was immune from arrest while in office. However, Vruomanh and his supporters badly wanted to have Riyannah locked up and interrogated. Again her uncle saved the day. He threatened that if anything happened to Riyannah he would fly to every other city on Kanan and tell them what was going on in Mestar. Nothing short of death would stop him.

"I was safe after that. But you weren't. It was obvious that Vruomanh wanted to capture you alive. It was just as obvious that if you didn't do what he wanted, he would see that you were killed in an 'accident.' I had to make sure you didn't fall into his hands."

That might have been impossible, without the help of the Menel ambassador. Taking matters into his own claws, he called up his own personal starship and made sure it followed Vruomanh everywhere the Councilor went. That was fortunate, both for Blade and for Kanan.

"When the Menel showed they were ready to fight to save you, the crew of Vruomanh's own ship overpowered him," said Riyannah. "He's now back in the same tower where you were held, and his guards are going to be more alert than yours were."

"What will happen to him?"

"He'll lose his seat on the Council at once. Then he will probably have his mental patterns altered so he can never even conceive of a violent act again. He will also lose his rights as a citizen of Mestar and become a *Yarash*—a Lone One, who can live nowhere on Kanan for more than a year at a time." No wonder Vruomanh might have preferred a beating. "Now the whole matter is coming before the Council of Kanan."

"All twenty Cities?"

"No. In an emergency, any six Cities can form a War Council and act for the others for half a year."

"I'm glad somebody on Kanan finally realizes this is an emergency."

Riyannah frowned. "Blade, that's not quite fair. You can recognize a war crisis because your people fight all the time. That doesn't make you so superior to us, and I'd wish you'd stop talking as if you were. I can ignore it, but I don't think the Council will care to hear it. If you want a chance to help us you won't get it by insulting us."

Blade had to admit she was right. He shouldn't grumble at the Kananites any more, particularly when he owed Riyannah and her uncle so much. However—

"Riyannah, I apologize, and I'll try to control my tongue before the Council. But I can't help wondering if we've wasted enough time to let Loyun Chard finish *Dark Warrior*. What happens then?"

There really wasn't any answer to that question.

The War Council met three days later. It was not only the first War Council to meet on Kanan in more than three centuries, it was the first to include the Menel. In addition to delegates from the Councils of six Cities, the Menel ambassador was on hand along with three of his staff. Everyone was plugged into a Speaker mounted in the center of the table.

"He insisted on it," said Riyannah's uncle. "If we did not let him sit on the Council, he would send a full report of what happened to his government. If the Menel thought we of Kanan were going to be slow and stupid in preparing to meet the Targans, they would start arming by themselves. They would arm heavily, fight the war, and perhaps win it without our help. Even if they did not win the war outright, their new fleet would make them stronger than Kanan. Then the alliance between us might break, and would certainly have to be changed."

Blade knew it wouldn't be tactful to suggest this might not be a bad thing, particularly to Yu Hardannah. However, it was obvious that Kanan would neither treat other worlds as full equals nor conquer them outright. They'd got away with this for so long only through receiving more cooperation from the Menel than they deserved. The Targan war was going to break that pattern, no matter what Blade did.

After that he concentrated on getting the War Council to move against the Targans and refused to worry about other matters of high interstellar politics. It was easy to work out his plan, and it came out smoothly and clearly when he spoke to the War Council.

"The first thing we must do is defend the asteroid base in the Targan system. More warships must be stationed there, hurd-ray projectors mounted on the surface, people unable to fight evacuated, food, water, and oxygen stored.

"However, none of this will be enough. Loyun Chard's great starship must be nearly finished by now. The attack will come before we can hope to strengthen the asteroid

129

base enough. Then the base will be destroyed. We will no longer be able to observe or attack Targa or help the underground in its fight against Chard. They may give up their fight. We cannot betray men and women who have risked their lives to help us, or leave Chard with a united planet behind him.

"So we must find a way to destroy the starship. Chard had poured men and material into building *Dark Warrior*, starving the rest of his military effort. If we destroy the ship, Targa will be helpless in space for years. Men and metal can be replaced, but not lost years.

"During these years we can build up our fleet—" his glance took in the Menel as well as the Kananites "—and the Targan underground can win support. Chard himself may die or be overthrown, and our own planets will be safe."

"How is the starship to be destroyed?" said one of the Menel. Engraved bracelets on all four arms showed he was of the Warrior Goran, probably the equivalent of a military attaché to the ambassador. "From what we have learned, it is much too strong to be attacked in space with the ships we have now."

"True. But the underground on Targa may be able to find a way to destroy it from within." He turned to Riyannah. "The underground has friends among the scientists and engineers at some of Chard's space bases, don't they?"

Riyannah nodded. "They have even won over some of the shuttle pilots who fly men and equipment up to the starship in orbit." She hesitated briefly. "They also told me they had plans of *Dark Warrior*. I didn't see the plans before I had to escape, but I think they were telling the truth."

"So the underground seems to have everything needed to enter the starship and destroy it from within," said Blade. "I suggest that we send a small mission to Targa with equipment and weapons to help them carry out the attack. It will take only a few people and one ship. It will also take less time than anything else we can do against *Dark Warrior*."

"You, of course, would be part of this mission?" said the Councilor from the City of Quinda.

"I think I am certainly one of the best people for it," said Blade. "You know that my people are warlike and

130

that I have been trained in war skills almost since I was a child. I do not say this makes me a good man or a wise man, but I think it makes me the right man for this mission."

"Perhaps it does," said the Councilor. "But it also makes you a brother in spirit to the Targans. How can we be sure you aren't proposing this mission so that you can then cause it to fail? If we let everything depend on this mission and you destroy, what happens after that? Then—"

The Councilor didn't get any farther. "You fool!" snapped Yu Hardannah. Riyannah looked as if she wanted to leap across the table and attack the Councilor. The Menel ambassador's claws were clicking angrily.

Blade rose and glared across the table at the Councilor from Quinda. "If you know that much about me, you know more. You know how much I hate people like Loyun Chard and his soldiers.

"You know that my own planet has suffered from people like them. You know that while I may not think much of the way the Kananites are running this war—"

At that point all the Menel burst into the hooting and whistling that was their laughter. Blade stopped, realizing he'd done exactly what he'd promised Riyannah not to do—insulting and abusing the Kananites. He found he didn't care. If the Kananites wouldn't help him carry out this mission, he'd ask the Menel and the Kananites be damned!

Eventually the chairman of the War Council restored something like order and allowed Blade to continue. "I will submit to another brain probe, if you wish, since you do not seem to trust the results of the first one. But I hope you will decide we do not need to waste that much time. I am an enemy of Loyun Chard. I will be until I die. I hope that is enough for you."

"It is," said the chairman. "But—may I ask how you plan to get aboard the ship and destroy it?"

Blade shook his head. "I wish I could tell you, but I can't make any detailed plans until I've talked with our Targan friends." Privately he suspected the attack on the starship would be a one-way mission, no matter how it was done. They might even be reduced to ramming it with one of the shuttlecraft. That would at least delay *Dark*

Warrior's first mission by several priceless months, even though it might not be fatal to anyone except the crew of the shuttlecraft. He saw no point in mentioning any of this. He was a barbarian warrior in the eyes of most of these people, except for the Menel and possibly Riyannah. If he talked about ramming the starship, they might think he was too mad to be trusted.

That was the end of any argument against carrying out the mission or having Blade lead it. The Council moved on to details, and once more politics reared its stubborn head. Should people from all six Cities represented on the Council be sent on the mission? That would mean taking the time to choose them. Or should they send the first half-dozen people who came to hand? That would mean only the Cities of those people would have any share of the credit for the victory. Was it wise?

After listening to an hour of this nonsense, Blade was ready to pound his head against the wall or pick up a chair and start pounding Councilors over their heads. The Kananites wouldn't give up "politics as usual" even if the Day of Judgment was staring them in the face. He noticed the Menel ambassador's claws clicking again and Riyannah's face turning grim.

Before matters could build to another explosion, Blade decided to interrupt. "I've been thinking this over. If I can have just one reliable person to help me, I think I can do everything necessary. If you can send the equipment and weapons to give to the Targans—"

"I'll come with you," said Riyannah. "The Targans already know me, so I won't have to win their trust. Also I already know the weapons we'll be using."

Before Blade could thank Riyannah, the Councilor from Quinda intervened once more. "You are of Mestar," he said sharply, looking at Riyannah. "What is more, you have done some questionable things in this affair already. Can we trust you? Even if we can, do we wish to give Mestar all the glory in this—?"

This time the Menel ambassador's claws reached out toward the Councilor. He got himself under control just before the claws closed on the man's throat. All the other Menel were hooting like sirens and bubbling like stewpots. The Speaker wasn't translating any of it, but from the tone

132

Blade suspected they were all cursing Kanan and the Kananites.

Blade picked up his water glass and banged it on the table to get silence. Then he nodded to Riyannah.

"I am quite willing to give up my rights as a citizen of Mestar," she said quietly. "I will become a Yarash, a Lone One, with no City to call my own for more than a year at a time. That way no one can say Mestar has won this victory. Now will it be safe to send me to Targa with Blade?" If her eyes had been lasers, the Councilor from Quinda would have been fried in his chair.

"Riyannah—" began her uncle, his face twisting in surprise and pain. She shook her head.

"No. There must be an end to this nonsense. Can we do nothing like sensible beings? You've said we can't trust this warrior Blade. I wonder what he could say about not trusting stubborn fools?" She went on like that for quite a while. By the time she ran out of breath, Blade didn't need to say anything. Riyannah had said it all for him.

"I think Riyannah and I can do the job," said Blade, when he could speak again. "But more is needed to earn the trust of the Targans. Riyannah told me you have promised to give them some of your science and technology, after they've helped you defeat Loyun Chard. Is this correct?"

The chairman and several other Councilors nodded slowly. "I don't think you've done the right thing. Consider. The Targans are a proud people who have suffered much. Many of those who follow Loyun Chard do so because they honestly believe in his promises to put an end to that suffering.

"In spite of this the underground holds out against Chard. They hope to defeat him and give Targa a better government. How can they promise anything better without some of your science and technology *already in their hands?*" Blade slapped both hands down on the table with pistol-shot cracks. Several of the Councilors started. "Yes! Suppose they have to go to their fellow Targans and say—help us overthrow Loyun Chard, because the Kananites have promised us some of their knowledge after we win? *Promises!*" Blade made the word sound like an obscenity.

He went on more softly. "Even the underground may

not believe you. They've been fighting Chard since before they ever heard of Kanan, losing friends, starving in the forest, always on the run, never sleeping soundly. If anybody in the whole galaxy has been fighting your battles, it's them. I think they have a right to more than promises."

He smiled. "I'm not asking you to give them the secrets of the hurd-ray or the Zin Field. But what about the solar collectors, the power cells, the anti-gravity generators, the Teacher Globes? I think they deserve some of that." He rose. "I won't ask you to answer me now. I won't even ask to listen to the discussion. This is a matter for you and the Menel, not for me. I must have an answer soon, though, and if that answer is 'No,' I don't know how much you can expect from the Targans."

He turned to Riyannah and offered her his arm. Together they swept out of the Council room, like a king and queen leaving an unruly court behind them. A buzz of conversation was rising as the door slid shut.

"Blade," said Riyannah softly, "I sincerely hope your people are in some other Dimension a long way off and stay there. You frighten even me, and as for those poor Councilors—" She shook her head.

"Do you think I've frightened them too much?"

"No. Just enough." She slid her arm through his and they walked off down the corridor.

Riyannah was right. The War Council called them back the next day to listen to the chairman propose a bargain.

"We admit that it is just to give the Targans certain items of our technology at once. It is quite likely this will help win their trust and cooperation."

It will also help them become independent more quickly, thought Blade. *Trying to make the Targans clients like the Menel won't work, and there will be a bloody shambles if you even try. Much better if you don't have the chance to try.* His attention returned to the chairman.

"—a warrior people," the man was saying. "There is no way we can send our knowledge to the Targans without also giving it to you, and to your people if you return to them. We do not know how your people will use such knowledge. You may end your wars and live in peace forever, as we have done. You may also become as great a menace to the universe as the Targans under Loyun

134

Chard. We cannot afford to leave ourselves defenseless, so we must ask you to help us.

"You have traveled across an aspect of reality that is neither time nor space. We have learned much about how you did this. We need to know more. We believe that other knowledge lies buried in your brain, at levels we cannot reach without your cooperation unless we are willing to endanger your sanity. We wish you no harm, so we ask your cooperation. Let us probe your brain again for all the knowledge you have of how to travel into Dimension X.

"Then we will give you all the information that is necessary to build the solar collectors and power cells. We will implant the information in your body so that only you will know it is there and only you can remove it. We will ask only that you get some agreement from the Targans before you give it to them."

The chairman rambled on for a while after that. Blade only listened with half an ear. He'd heard the important thing: the Kananites were asking him to give up the Dimension X secret, in return for their scientific knowledge to give to the Targans and then take Home if he could.

Blade's first reaction was a mental shout of: *Not until your sun goes nova!* Behind that shout were years of living with the Official Secrets Act and the knowledge of what leaking the Dimension X secret could do. He also remembered the sensations of the Zin Field transition across the light-years. Something in that Transition was too close to the trip into Dimension X for comfort. The Kananites might be halfway to the Dimension X secret without even knowing it. If they picked his brains and learned everything there, how much farther could they go? Certainly they had computers far beyond Lord Leighton's. The risks were enormous.

On the other hand, what about the certainties? If he didn't go along with the Council's proposal, Loyun Chard's war would become inevitable. Whatever else happened, millions of beings, Kananite, Targan, and Menel, would die. If Loyun Chard won, a Targan empire would spread across this Dimension, perhaps discovering the Dimension X secret on its own and then spreading blood and ruin even farther.

Even if Loyun Chard was defeated, the Menel and the

135

Kananites would bear the scars for generations. The Targans might be completely destroyed, and they would certainly end up confined to their own impoverished planet, bitter and vengeful.

Either way this Dimension would pay a grim price for Blade's refusal.

And the risks of revealing the Dimension X secret— were they really so great? Blade began to wonder. They could not get out of his brain more knowledge than was already there. All he knew was what the Project had done so far—randomly shooting a single naked man off into Dimension X. Even if the Kananites learned how to do that much at once, it would hardly make them a greater inter-Dimensional menace.

If they did learn more eventually, that might be serious. It would take a while, though. The Menel would not appreciate being left out, and that meant taking time to develop Dimension X travel techniques suited to Menel brains. Then there would be a host of political problems to be solved, and Blade knew far too well how long it took the Kananites to deal with these.

It might be generations before the Kananites could become any sort of menace, even if they wanted to. By that time Home Dimension Earth would either be in such bad shape it needed Kananite help or advance so far the Kananites would be no danger to it.

No. He could not condemn millions of people to death by refusing this proposal. Not when there was so little chance that anything really dangerous would come of accepting it. He had to live with the Official Secrets Act, but he also had to live with himself.

Blade straightened up, and felt as if all the millions of prospective war dead were joining in his sigh of relief. The chairman was looking at him.

"Mr. Chairman, Kananites and Menel of this War Council, I agree to the proposal."

This time everybody was applauding, Riyannah was embracing him, and the Menel ambassador was practically dancing around the room, waving all four arms over his head.

Chapter 19

Once they'd made up their minds to act, the Kananites showed they could move fast enough. Like a boulder pried loose after many hours' hard work, events now went rolling and crashing along.

Blade spent three days having his brain intensively probed. It left him with the worst headaches he'd ever had in his life, as if somebody was hitting him over the skull with a dull ax. He didn't have the vaguest memories of what he might have revealed. Kananite doctors watched him carefully, the Menel ambassador watched the doctors, and after two days in bed he was fully recovered.

He recovered just in time to have the technical data planted in his body. The doctors placed the films along the inside of his thigh, under a layer of tough but completely natural-looking artificial skin. It didn't restrict his movements at all, even in bed with Riyannah, but it gave complete protection to the films. Any time he wanted to, he could dissolve the skin with a special spray, let someone look at the films, then put them back and apply more skin. Blade was rather sorry he hadn't known about this artificial skin before and had information about it put on the films. Back in Home Dimension it would be a blessing to people with severe burns or skin diseases.

After that Blade started collecting the load of gear he would be taking to Targa for his mission: hurd-ray projectors, power cells, explosives, electronic devices, everything else he'd need to make fifty Targans into super-soldiers. Much of the equipment was Menel-manufactured. Blade detected the ambassador's fine claw in this and wondered why. Was the ambassador simply trying to save time? Or was he trying to hint to the Targan underground that the Menel might be better friends than the Kananites? Blade didn't really care. All he cared about now was getting

back to Targa and starting to work on the project of blowing Loyun Chard's great starship into the smallest possible
pieces.

Before he boarded the ship for Targa, Blade had one
other discussion. In many ways it was the most useful
hour he'd spent in this Dimension, and he spent it with a
Menel.

The Menel was short, less than seven feet tall, and
elderly, his arms stiff and his skin turning brown like an
autumn leaf. He also was one of the most brilliant scientists of his people and head of the scientific section of the
Menel embassy here on Kanan.

The Mendel stooped in a way that made him seem almost hunched and he spoke rapidly, in an unusually high-
pitched voice and with many gestures. There were times
during the conversation when Blade could have closed his
eyes and sworn he was talking to Lord Leighton. Certainly
he was talking to the same type of mind and personality,
even if it was housed in a body like a giant stalk of asparagus. It was a pity that Lord Leighton and the Menel
scientist would never meet.

The discussion was mostly about Blade's previous meetings with the Menel and what they implied. "The ones
who made the Ice Dragons—I do not think it is needed, to
worry about them," said the Menel. "As you describe the
explosion, they could not have survived it."

"I thought so," said Blade. "But why did they make the
Ice Dragons in the first place?"

The scientist's gesture was the Menel equivalent of a
shrug. "Who is to be certain, now they are dead. It is
known that the leaders of Menel expeditions sometimes go
mad. One out of a thousand, no more, but it has happened. Sometimes they even find the crew is behind them,
not fighting them. We try to find ways that it will not happen again, and the Kananites help us. So far—no success." Another shrug.

The discussion turned to Blade's other meeting with the
Menel, where they'd been sending the birds and sea beasts
against the human inhabitants of a Dimension slowly vanishing under a rising sea. The scientist agreed with Blade's
guess that it was a case of a shipwrecked expedition trying
to do the best it could with limited resources.

"I do not say what they did to the people or even the

animals is good," he said. "Yet—we Menel cannot live well too close to water, with air too wet. They needed land on the continents, not just on their island. The people you have described—they would not make peace with those shaped like us. Or do you think otherwise?"

Blade had to admit the scientist was right. Even highly civilized people could fly into a panic over minor differences of skin color. Tribes of barbarians seeing a Menel would shoot first and not ask questions at all.

"When they have some land of their own, they will try to make peace with the humans and help them. Otherwise they could only sit down on their island and die."

The scientist hesitated, then went on in a tone Blade recognized even through the electronic translation of the Speaker. It was the tone of a scientist who will not pretend to knowledge he doesn't have.

"At least—these things I have said would be so, if the Menel you met were the Menel of this Dimension. I do not think both of them were. I would say that the Menel who made the Ice Dragons were of a Dimension in which they were rulers and conquerors of space and stars. Perhaps there never were Kananites, or perhaps the Menel were the masters."

Blade swallowed. "And the Menel of the water world?"

"It is not impossible they were my people. They seem to be very much like them. Certainly starships disappear at times. Who knows if they do not pass into another Dimension, where the world they seek is not as they expect? But I think they also are a different Menel, less different than those of the Ice Dragons but still not my people."

The scientist went on, painting a mind-freezing picture of a reality consisting of an infinite number of Dimensions, each of which might be infinite in space. The idea had occurred to Blade, but he found it hard to sit calmly and hear someone else discuss it as a real possibility.

"I don't reject this," he said finally. "In fact it's much the simplest explanation. Among other things, it means I haven't been getting bounced around in space as well as in Dimension. But if there is this infinity of infinities, why did I end up three times in Dimensions with Menel in them?"

"If I knew that answer, I would be much closer to that Dimension X secret you would be happy we did not have," said the scientist. "I do not. I have only the theory, that Dimensions which have things in common—"

"Such as Menel?"

"Yes. Or your race, which you have always found in Dimension X. These Dimensions with things in common—they are closer together than Dimensions which have other life or no life at all. I think the Dimension where you met the Wizard of Rentoro must have been the closest one of all, so close he could pass into it by his mind strength alone."

Blade laughed. The Menel scientist's words gave him a picture of reality as a huge vinyard, with each grape a Dimension and each bunch of grapes a cluster of Dimensions with something in common. In some bunches the link was the Menel, in others humans, in others Kananites, in others beings who breathed hydrogen, saw by infrared, and had twelve tentacles, in still others things beyond imagining.

It was a weird picture, but then any picture of a reality that was infinite in several different ways at once couldn't be anything else. Once again Blade was glad he hadn't tried to become a scientist. He simply didn't have whatever was needed to make a person able to deal with this sort of concept day after day. His talents ran more to dealing with the practical problems of one Dimension at a time.

Lord Leighton, on the other hand, was going to have fun with this picture. Perhaps "fun" wasn't the right word. It raised an ugly question: was any reliable sort of inter-Dimension travel ever going to be possible? If it wasn't, what would be left to justify Project Dimension X? It was far too expensive to keep going as a pure research project, although Lord Leighton would still fight for it like a mother bear for her cubs.

There could be a nasty homecoming ahead, Blade realized. First, though, came the comparatively straightforward job of removing Loyun Chard's starship from this Dimension. Lord Leighton could take his turn.

Blade ended the discussion with the Menel scientist as soon as he politely could. Then he ordered several bottles of wine and called up Riyannah. He wanted a lot of both to help him get back in touch with the one reality around him.

Blade and Riyannah returned to Targa in a Kananite ship. Riyannah was now disguised as a Targan. The best doctors and surgeons on Kanan did the work, but even so it wasn't completely successful. Her hair was now dark and close-cropped but still too fine for any Targan's. Artificial skin fastened the last two fingers of each hand together into an awkward bundle but couldn't completely hide the extra joints. Chemical injections changed her skin and eye color to something that just possibly might have been Targan. There was nothing anybody could do about her slimness.

Fortunately she didn't have to fool the underground, because she never could. Blade wasn't even sure she'd be able to fool the enemy, "unless the light is weak and they're in a hurry or too drunk to see straight," as he put it. He still didn't object, since Riyannah wanted it this way. She had almost enough reasons to justify risking her neck.

"I'm an observer for the War Council, and how can I do my job if I can't go where I can observe? Besides, you may need another pair of eyes and ears and another gun for dealing with the underground. You've said it yourself—'Bare is the back that has no brother to defend it.' Perhaps a sister will do as well."

"If that sister is you, she will," said Blade. He hoped things would work out so that Riyannah didn't have to follow him every inch of the way. Otherwise nothing short of locking her up would keep her out of danger.

They made the return trip considerably faster than they'd made the trip out. The captain was pushing both the ship and the passengers to their limits. After the first Transition Riyannah was unconscious for six hours and Blade was disoriented for half the next day. After that they both put away their pride and took the other three Transitions to Targa under drugs.

They spent several days on the asteroid base. Blade noticed two welcome signs that someone was taking the danger of war seriously. A Menel starship came in and unloaded a dozen short-range patrol ships. A big Kananite ship loaded several hundred civilians and all their baggage, then left for home.

On the sixth day another Kananite ship unloaded the interplanetary craft that would take Blade and Riyannah the

141

rest of the way to Targa. She was small, sleek, heavily armored, and bristling with hurd-ray projectors and missile launchers. Her crew were proud of their ship and ready for a fight against the Targans. They were almost disappointed when Blade told them their mission on this trip was to sneak in without being detected.

"Don't worry, you'll get plenty of fighting if we fail," Blade said. "Maybe if we succeed." He looked at the ship again and at the two men and three women who made up her crew. They were the first Kananites other than Riyannah he'd ever met who seemed to enjoy the prospect of a fight. He could almost believe he was listening to some Home Dimension fighter pilots, all determined to become aces in their first battle.

"How many ships are there like *Trenbar?*" he asked.

"Only three or four ready for space," said the captain. "We're the first one out here. I think there are five or six more building at home."

Three or four! Blade looked at *Trenbar* again. He'd never seen a spacecraft with "warship" written so clearly all over her. If he and Riyannah and the Targans could give Kanan the time to build three or four hundred like *Trenbar* and train crews for them all, Kanan and the Menel could thumb their noses at anything Loyun Chard could do.

Blade's optimism suffered a rude shock when he and Riyannah finally landed among the fighters of the Targan underground.

The trip itself was everything *Trenbar's* captain promised. They came in over the uninhabited north polar continent and hedge-hopped all the way south to their landing place without being attacked. Once a Targan plane started closing on them, but the captain accelerated and left the plane behind as if it was anchored in the sky. They slipped down through a mountain pass and landed less than a hundred miles from where Blade and Riyannah first met. The Targans helped unload the equipment, then *Trenbar* stood on her tail and leaped into the sky vanishing in a thunderclap of torn air.

Blade and Riyannah were taken to the current main base of the underground, in a maze of limestone caves deep in the mountains. There they confronted the five surviving leaders of the underground who'd been able to make it to this rendezvous. Chard's planes and men were pulling back now, but there'd been a period of savage raids after Blade and Riyannah escaped. Of the twelve leaders Riyannah expected to meet, four were dead and three more didn't dare leave their hiding places to travel to this meeting. Hundreds of the underground's fighters and many of their weapons and key pieces of equipment were also gone. This only strengthened their suspicions of Kananite and Kananite help.

Blade and Riyannah did their best, but for a while it seemed that their best wasn't going to be good enough. The Targans twisted everything they said, asked questions even the War Council of Kanan couldn't have answered, and generally made trouble.

At least Blade felt they were making trouble. He did his best not to let that feeling run away with him, because he knew it wasn't true. The Targan underground was battered, desperate, and sullen. They knew that Kananite aid might save them, but they also knew that Kananite treachery would finish them off like a moth dropped into a laser beam. They couldn't decide if it was worth risking the treachery in order to get the aid.

Blade understood all this, sympathized, and still began to feel like knocking the leaders' heads together. If there was one thing they couldn't do, it was refuse to make up their minds until Loyun Chard made the decision for them. At the same time Blade knew he couldn't push too hard, make a nuisance of himself, or arouse anyone's suspicions. Unlike the Kananites, the Targans wouldn't hesitate a minute in shooting troublemakers.

Eventually Blade saw that he had no choice, and Riyannah agreed with him. The War Council might object, but it was thirty light-years away on Kanan. He and Riyannah were here on Targa, facing Targans who were getting more stubborn and even threatening each day. They weren't going to risk throwing everything away merely to keep the Council happy.

So Blade removed the artificial skin, then appeared before the Targans with the technical films in his hand.

"Here is everything you need to know for making the Kananites' power cells and solar converters. Once you put these in production, Targa's energy problems will soon be solved. You can go before your fellow Targans and tell them that Loyun Chard leads them to war only to satisfy his own ambitions. There is no more need to conquer other planets among the stars and loot them or die by the millions trying to do so. All they need to do is overthrow Chard, then turn their factories from making planes and lasers to making these." He dropped the films on the table in front of the leaders.

For a while Blade wondered if he'd made a mistake. Some of the leaders seemed to favor an agreement. Others went on muttering suspiciously. Since one of the things they muttered was "holding that Kananite bitch Riyannah as a hostage," Blade decided to leave.

As he headed toward the door, two of the leaders drew their guns and things got rather lively. Blade shot one man in the leg and clubbed another with the butt of his own pistol. Riyannah tripped up a third, then hit him over the head with a chair. Before anyone else could move, Blade and Riyannah were out of sight, on their way to the cave where their equipment was stored.

They reached the cave, left a message outside, then closed the door and fused it shut with a hurd-ray blast. The message read:

> Targans,
> Study the films and see if we are telling the truth. If you think we are not giving you enough, say so. We will be happy to talk about giving you more.
> But we will not come out until you are ready to talk, one way or another. If you try to break down the door, we will blow up this cave, along with all of your supplies, most of you, and ourselves. We are very tired of trying to be polite to people who do not understand that we all have only one enemy—Loyun Chard.
>
> Richard Blade
> Sar Riyannah

Riyannah signed the message, but she looked hard at Blade before she did so. "Would you really blow up this cave and everything in it?"

144

"Not really. There are ways we can keep ourselves out of the underground's hands without doing them real damage."

"You're bluffing?"

"More or less. But they don't know it, and they can't afford to risk finding out the hard way."

Inside the cave they pulled out mattresses and blankets, dropped them beside the piled gear, and settled down to wait. The cave was warm, heated by an underground hot spring, and Blade pulled off his tunic and shirt. Riyannah looked at him for a moment, then jumped up and disappeared around the pile of gear.

She was back in a moment with a small package wrapped in an exotic Kananite fabric with luminous embroidery. She placed it in Blade's lap.

"Should I open it now?" he asked.

"Yes. I'd meant to wait until we were taking off for the starship. But those people out there might be angry enough to break down the door. I want you to have it now, so—" She shrugged, and Blade mentally filled in the rest of the sentence, "—so you can be wearing it if we have to make our last fight here."

Blade unwrapped the package. It held a bracelet of Kanan's woven metal, lighter than aluminum but stronger than steel, inlaid with patterns of dust-sized jewels. Across the top was a black band that seemed to absorb light. Blade put the bracelet on, then saw faint shapes begin to glow within the blackness. The glow brightened, the shapes flowed and shimmered, then they joined into one and Blade was looking at a full-length portrait of a nude Riyannah.

He raised his head, to see Riyannah lying on her mattress, head propped on one hand, as nude as her portrait. "In the black band are more jewels, arranged to make the picture of me. The heat of your body makes them glow."

"Yes, and the heat of your body can make me glow." Riyannah laughed, as Blade stood up and began slipping off his trousers.

The Targans came the next morning, when both Blade and Riyannah were still comfortably asleep in each other's arms. They woke up quickly enough when they learned

145

that the Targans were ready to make peace and start planning.

There was still more talking, but no more nonsense. The leader Riyannah had hit with the chair attended, his head bandaged, but Blade's two victims didn't. Blade never saw either of them again and suspected it wouldn't be tactful to ask what happened to them.

In any case he and Riyannah were much too busy. First he had to retrieve the technical films as soon as the Targans were through copying them, then replace them on his thigh and cover them again with artificial skin. Then there were days of studying the plans of *Dark Warrior*, maps of enemy bases, lists of underground bands and their available weapons—a dozen different kinds of paper, piling higher each day. They talked with the underground's leaders, with various scientists, engineers, and spaceship pilots who'd fled from Chard's bases, and with a dozen men and women who'd led the underground's field teams in combat.

Then Blade and the team leaders picked fifty of the best fighters on hand, and the serious training for the attack on the starship began.

Chapter 20

A steady drizzling rain was falling. Water dripped from the trees above as Blade crawled through bushes on his hands and knees. Riyannah was close behind, moving almost as silently as Blade.

They came to the end of the bushes. A few scattered trees lay ahead, then open country fading off into the rainy darkness. In that darkness a string of lights glowed a pale orange. They were the lights of Station Four, Blade's target and the first step on the way to the starship.

Still on their hands and knees, Blade and Riyannah reached the nearest tree. No sight or sound of any alarm, and visibility was getting steadily worse.

That wouldn't be all to the good. It would make the fighting in the station confused and risky, if the guards didn't go down at the first rush. It could also delay the reinforcements needed to move on to the next stage of the plan.

On the other hand, the rainy night would be perfect cover. The first attackers would certainly be hard to see and hear until it was too late. The sentries would be thinking mostly of the rain trickling down the backs of their necks and squelching in their boots. Even the best of Loyun Chard's soldiers didn't care for bad weather, and these sentries wouldn't be among the best. As far as Chard was concerned, the underground was on the run, too crippled to be a danger even to isolated shuttlecraft bases like Station Four. So why waste good men guarding it, far off in land that hadn't been settled since the Great War?

The rain would also make Blade's own job a good deal easier. Station Four had to be taken completely by surprise and captured before any messages could reach the outside world. There were two ways such messages could go out. One was by laser beam to a communications satel-

147

lite high overhead, the other was by radio. The rain and overcast would make the laser virtually useless, so Blade now had only one target. If he could smash the radio station before anyone gave the alarm, Station Four would be unable to call for help or send out a warning.

Slowly Blade stood up. He was wearing Targan uniform, with a major's insignia. On his back was a conventional Targan field pack with unconventional contents. It held several charges of Kananite explosive, each the equivalent of more than half a ton of TNT. It also held a compact hurd-ray projector, small enough to fire with one hand but powerful enough to burn through several inches of steel.

Riyannah also stood up, unhooked a Targan helmet from her belt, and handed it to Blade. He put it on and tightened the chinstrap.

"How do I look?"

"You look enough like one of those piles of dung to make me shudder," she said. She was wearing Targan uniform herself, with a sergeant's insignia. She might even pass for a Targan as long as the rain kept falling and the enemy's soldiers were too busy to look closely.

"Good," said Blade. "That should get me inside, and there's half the battle. All I need to worry about on the way in is meeting some officer with more rank." He gripped Riyannah by both shoulders and kissed her. "Don't let anyone get too close while I'm knocking out the lights. It's going to be chancy shooting even with the projector."

"We'll be careful if you will," she said. Then Blade turned and strode out from behind the tree toward the light of Station Four.

The plan for destroying the starship *Dark Warrior* was mostly Blade's creation. With the information the underground gave him, he was able to work out a much better one than they'd been able to do. The underground people were brave and intelligent, but they didn't have Blade's years of experience against opponents far tougher than the soldiers of Loyun Chard.

Several basic facts shaped the plan. First, *Dark Warrior* was so heavily escorted that she would have to be attacked by stealth. No suspicious ship could hope to get within

148

ramming distance or even missile range. That ruled out the simplest and most ruthless form of attack—a straightforward kamikaze mission.

So the attackers would have to slip a boarding party into the ship. Fifteen or twenty armed men with hurd-rays and explosives could wreck the ship beyond repair. They might even be able to escape afterward in the confusion. The problem would be getting them on board in the first place, then keeping them alive long enough to finish their work.

The Targans threw in an extra requirement that made things more difficult. They did not want *Dark Warrior* attacked while she was in orbit around Targa. They wanted the boarding party to wait until the ship was millions of miles out in space on her way to the asteroids. As one leader said to Blade:

"If we cripple the ship far out in space, she will never get home." Neither would the boarding party, Blade thought, but decided not to mention that. "If we cripple her in orbit, the missiles and lasers will still survive. *Dark Warrior* will become a gigantic orbiting fortress, able to strike down from space at any point on the planet. Even if Chard can no longer threaten the Kananites, he will be able to threaten his own people. He may also turn *Dark Warrior's* weapons loose on our hiding places. If we lose too many more people, we cannot hope to do much even after Chard is overthrown. We will only be one fraction in a civil war, and not the strongest one either."

In spite of these plausible arguments, Blade's first reaction was to tell the Targans, "You're all crazy!" Then he thought the matter over and realized they had a point. The starship had to be taken out of Targan politics as well as interstellar politics. The underground could not be asked to suffer more than it had already, and Targa could not be condemned to a long, bloody, and pointless civil war that could only leave the planet a wreck. Some of the Kananites might not mind seeing Targa dissolve in such a war, but Blade would have no part of that idea.

There were also some real advantages to waiting. If the boarding party could lie low until *Dark Warrior* was within range of the patrol ships around the asteroid base, they might have help. The patrol ships might not be able to do much damage but they would certainly distract the starship's crew. After the fighting was over, the patrol ships could also take off any survivors of the boarding party.

Blade saw one more advantage of waiting that he didn't mention. If a dozen or so intelligent Targans saw the asteroid base, they'd know far more about the Kananites and the Menel. They'd know too much to let the Kananites go back on any further promises of technical assistance. Blade still didn't trust Kanan's War Council and he'd be glad to do anything he could to take matters out of their hands.

The Targans' idea of having the boarding party wait until *Dark Warrior* was deep in space would still have been suicidal, except for the way the ship was built. She bristled with lasers and missile launchers. She was also designed to carry more than two thousand soldiers and settlers to new planets, and huge cargoes of raw materials back to Targa. She had enough cabins to hold the population of a small town, and cargo holds large enough to swallow half a dozen smaller spaceships.

On the mission to destroy the asteroid base, the ship would be carrying only her fighting crew of three hundred men. Or so the underground had heard, from their spies in the space program.

"How reliable are these people?" asked Blade.

"Reliable enough so we're willing to risk the boarding party on their reports." The underground's leaders seldom gave away unnecessary information, and Blade respected them for that. The man hesitated. "There may be more, but I don't think they'll be fighting men. The last report said that one block of cabins is being fitted up luxuriously, but it won't hold more than fifty or sixty people."

It sounded to Blade as if some of the VIP's in Loyun Chard's space program and armed forces were inviting themselves along for the ride. So much the better. The boarding party could blow a large hole in the upper ranks of Chard's government as well as in his precious starship.

In any case, there would be plenty of room left in the starship's cabins and holds. If the boarding party could get on board without arousing suspicion, there was a good chance they'd be able to hide until the time came to strike. Blade doubted that the ship's crew would even know all the compartments and cabins aboard, let alone bother inspecting them regularly. A boarding party hiding itself snugly aboard their magnificent and invincible starship would be about the last danger the crew would think of.

So there it was: Blade's plan. Capture one of the ground bases for the orbital shuttlecraft. Fly a shuttle up to the starship, meanwhile covering their tracks on the ground. Get the boarding party and its weapons aboard the ship, then hide them. Wait however long it took, in whatever discomfort they had to endure, until the starship headed out into space. Wait a little longer, then STRIKE.

Very simple—until the time came to carry it out.

Blade strode forward, trying to move silently. He expected to be spotted and challenged but he didn't want it happening too soon. Some trigger-happy sentry might shoot before challenging. Blade was wearing body armor of Kananite woven metal under his uniform, so even the heavy Targan slugs probably wouldn't hurt him. Shooting would almost certainly give the alarm, though, and that would be worse.

The rain pattered on Blade's helmet and drummed on the soft earth. He slogged through mud and splashed through puddles. Once he stopped to adjust the sling of his rifle, another time he stopped to make sure the throwing knife up his sleeve moved freely in its sheath.

Suddenly a beam of light danced across the ground toward him, then leaped up to shine in his face.

"Halt! Who goes there?"

Blade wanted to laugh. The orders of sentries seemed to be the same in every army in every Dimension he knew. He called back:

"Major Harbo, Military Inspector's Office. Glad to know you're on the alert."

There was a long silence. Blade used the time to spot the source of the light and walk toward it. As he'd expected, praising the sentry caught the man off balance.

Blade was only ten feet from the open gate when the sentry spoke again. "Sorry, sir. You'll still have to give the password."

Blade lowered his voice. "Not so loud, you idiot. I'm doing a security inspection on this station. You've passed, but I won't appreciate it if you alert all the other sentries."

"But—"

"Damn it, keep your voice down! You'll have all your friends thinking the underground is attacking!"

The sentry laughed—then died with the laugh stuck in his throat as Blade drove the knife into him. Blade held the man upright until he stopped kicking, then lowered him silently to the ground. He bent to pick up the sentry's flashlight, then stiffened as another figure loomed out of the darkness beyond the gate.

Blade knew he was caught red-handed and didn't even bother opening his mouth. He jerked his knife out of the body, caught it by the point, and threw. The approaching man reeled backward, rifle falling from his hands, the knife sticking out of his face. He started to scream, then Blade closed in and chopped him across the throat. Again Blade lowered a dead body to the ground and retrieved his knife.

Blade knew he had to move fast now. He pulled the hurd-ray projector out of his pack and used it on low power to cut most of the wires around the gate. Now it could no longer be closed. Then he stalked in through the gateway, projector held ready to fire.

To his right towered the launching platforms for the shuttlecraft. Two of the platforms were occupied. The shuttle-craft looked very much like the winged-disk jet planes, but were three times as big. In their bellies they carried anti-gravity units and in their tails racks of solid-fuel rockets to kick them into the air. The Targans' anti-gravity was less reliable than the Kananites' and could not safely be used within fifteen thousand feet of the ground.

No lights showed in the cockpits of the shuttles. That meant no one aboard to send out signals over the shuttles' radios. If Blade took out the main radio station, that should do the job.

The station with its hundred-foot mast was on the left, just under two hundred yards away. Light spilled out through the open door, illuminating a wide expanse of grass and concrete in front of the station. Blade saw two soldiers standing on the roof, a rocket launcher lying between them. Fortunately they were looking the other way. He crept to the edge of the illuminated area, looked in all directions, and saw nothing suspicious. Then he sprinted toward the open door.

The thud of his feet alerted the men on the roof. He

152

heard one of them shout as he came pounding up to the door. Then he was inside the radio building, pulling the door shut with one hand and raising the hurd-ray with the other. He was in a short corridor with doors opening off either side, leading to a large room filled with consoles and switchboards. Blade aimed the projector and fired a long burst, sweeping everything he could see. Metal cracked and melted, wiring shorted, threw sparks, and gushed smoke, heavy objects crashed to the floor, and voices started screaming, cursing, and shouting all at once.

Blade started down the corridor to catch the people in the room before they recovered from the surprise. A door to his right flew open and an officer with a drawn laser pistol popped out. The two men collided. The laser beam hissed past Blade and knocked a chunk out of the ceiling. Blade punched the officer in the stomach, then smashed the butt of the hurd-ray across the back of his neck. Blade leaped over the fallen man and charged into the main room.

Bullets flew past Blade as one of the radio operators swung in his seat and emptied a pistol. The bullets smashed more radio gear without touching Blade. Then the hurd-ray was sweeping along the consoles and all three radio operators slumped in their seats, two headless and one burned completely in two. Blade fired two more quick blasts to quiet the writhing bodies on the floor, then played the beam in a complete circle around him. By the time he'd finished, every recognizable piece of communications equipment in the room was half-melted junk. Blue and green smoke swirled like a fog and clawed at Blade's mouth and nose.

Breathing shallowly, he took out one of the bombs, set both the time fuse and the booby-trap, then shoved it out of sight under one of the bodies. The radio station had to be completely demolished, otherwise someone might still improvise an emergency signal by hooking a portable radio to the big mast on the roof.

The bomb was set. Blade flattened himself against the wall and crept back to the corridor. Voices sounded from the outer door. He pulled out a golf-ball sized blue grenade, armed it, and hurled it down the corridor. When the echoes from the explosion died away the voices were only fading moans. Blade got outside as fast as he could.

A rifle went off overhead as Blade broke into the open. One bullet hit him in the shoulder but his body armor kept it out of his flesh. He ducked, searching for the rifleman and raising his projector. The two soldiers on top of the radio building were alert and one was firing his rifle in all directions. The other had the rocket launcher on his shoulder and was peering around in search of a target. The area in front of the building was dark now that the lights inside were out, and neither man could see clearly.

Blade's night vision was a good deal better. He picked off the rifleman, then shifted aim to the soldier with the rocket launcher. The man moved just as Blade fired and the ray only burned off one leg. He screamed, hopped wildly about, then toppled off the roof, taking the launcher with him. Blade was about to dart forward and retrieve it when the bomb in the radio building went off prematurely.

The bomb he'd planted was the equivalent of more than a ton of TNT. The radio building vanished in a hurricane blast of smoke, flame, and hurtling wreckage. Blade went down again as if he'd been hit by a truck. He lay in the mud as the wreckage pattered and crashed down about him. The radio mast wavered, leaned to the right, and toppled over. Before the scream of twisting metal died away, Blade was on his feet again.

By now Blade had made enough noise to wake the dead, and everyone in Station Four had to be on the move. He sprinted back toward the fence, projector in one hand and a grenade in the other. Someone in a building to Blade's left foolishly switched on a light, silhouetting three helmeted figures. He hurled the grenade, heard glass smash, then the explosion and the screams.

The streets and alleys of Station Four were rapidly filling with running men, some in uniform, some half-dressed, some in pajamas, one or two stark naked. Officers shouted orders which made no sense and which weren't obeyed even when anyone heard them. No one paid any attention to Blade. He was in Targan uniform, he wasn't moving any faster than most of the other men, and it was too dark to recognize the ray projector in his hand.

Blade took advantage of the confusion to run even faster. Sooner or later even the half-trained and wholly panic-stricken Targan soldiers would sort themselves out enough to become dangerous opponents. The underground couldn't afford too many casualties among their attack group without fatally weakening the boarding party.

All the clothed men seemed to be in uniform. That meant the scientific and engineering people were staying under cover. Good. Several of them were underground supporters with key roles in the plan, and the underground had no real quarrel with the rest. No civilian of any sort had a place in this sort of firefight in any case.

Blade reached a spot where he had a clear line of fire to the perimeter lights and dropped to one knee. Sighting precisely, he picked off all the lights he could see, working from left to right. Eight—nine—ten—eleven—then the answering flare of hurd-rays blazed from the darkness beyond the perimeter. The rest of the attackers were coming in.

Blade jumped up and ran back into the station. As he ran he pulled a white armband from his belt pouch and tied it around his left arm. Both sides would be wearing Targan uniforms, but the underground's people would have white armbands. Blade hoped that would be enough to prevent fatal mistakes.

By the time Blade reached the center of the station he could hear a swelling battle roar from behind him. Hurd-rays crackled, rifles hammered, grenades thumped and crashed, men screamed in rage or pain. Blade kept running, leaped a drainage ditch, then slipped on the far bank and went to his knees.

A few yards away stood a rough sheet metal building. Beyond it lay the far perimeter of the station, its lights still burning. Metal clanged and a motor whined. The door of the building slid open, but no one was foolish enough to turn on a light. A six-wheeled flatbed truck rolled out of the door and turned toward Blade. Two men sat in the darkened cab, the driver and a gunner. Two more rode on the back, hanging on to the mounting of a heavy laser.

That truck had to be stopped. If it wasn't, it would get way in the darkness and the rain, then move on until it had clear weather. Then the laser could reach out to a communications satellite or even the starship. The surprise the underground desperately needed would be gone.

Blade aimed his hurd-ray and fired. The projector hissed faintly, glowed, then gushed smoke. Blade threw it down

155

and reached for a grenade. He was rising to throw it when someone in the building flicked on all the lights. Suddenly Blade was painfully visible as he balanced on the edge of the drainage ditch.

The driver of the truck jammed on the brakes and twisted the wheel. One of the men in back fired a pistol at Blade. The bullet spun him around as he hurled the grenade. It sailed over the truck and landed in the door of the building. All the lights went out but the truck kept going.

Blade took advantage of the darkness to spring after it. He broke every world's record for the ten-yard dash and was scrambling over the tail before the men in back saw him. The pistol banged again, the second man tried to raise his rifle, then Blade was on top of them.

He gripped the first man by his pistol arm, then wheeled to kick the second one in the groin. The second man flew off the truck, landed, and didn't get up. Blade twisted the pistol out of the first man's grip, then chopped him across the throat and threw his body after his comrade.

The truck lurched to a stop just inside the rear gate. Blade smashed the butt of the pistol down on the driver's head as he tried to scramble out of the cab. The other man ran off faster than Blade could follow, but a hurd-ray blast from the darkness took his legs out from under him just outside the gate. Blade looked around and saw Riyannah stepping out of the shadows, putting a fresh power cell into her projector.

"Good shot," he said, and clapped her on the shoulder. "Now get back. I'm going to put a grenade under this truck."

Riyannah shook her head. "You can save it. There aren't enough soldiers left to do anything with it."

"Everything under control?"

"Yes. We've got people in a truck out now, searching the area for runaways. The reinforcements are on their way in and—no, here they are now."

Propellers whirred overhead in the gloom. A searchlight cut through the base of the clouds, lighting up the two shuttlecraft. The light grew, then a troop carrier floated down out of the night to land between the two shuttles. Buildings cut off the view, but Blade knew that thirty more underground fighters would be scrambling out of the carrier to join the dying battle.

Blade and Riyannah stood briefly hand in hand as silence fell over Station Four. Then they walked back toward the shuttles. Before they'd gone very far they met a working party—six soldier prisoners in their underwear, two underground guards in uniform. The prisoners were pushing a wheeled rubbish bin already half filled with bits of wreckage.

"Moving on to the next stage already, I see," said Blade. The next stage was cleaning up Station Four so as to leave few signs of the night's battle for satellites or planes to discover.

"They'd better be," said Riyannah. "All we have to do is get through about fifty hours' work in the next ten. Then everything will be all right, for a little while."

Chapter 21

It actually took eleven hours to carry out the next stage of what the underground now called Plan Blade. They couldn't do anything about the fallen radio tower and the smashed radio building, but most of the other scars of battle were gone before dawn. The captive soldiers worked hard after two of them were shot for trying to escape.

Meanwhile the underground's space pilots and engineers were checking out one of the shuttles. This was a job that normally took several days. By cutting enough corners to make the pilots shudder, the job was done in six hours. The passenger compartment was fitted with seats and the boarding party's equipment loaded into the cargo hold along with a full shipment of legitimate cargo. At last everything was ready, down to the firing circuits for the solid-fuel boosters and the toilet paper in the zero-g bathroom aft.

Blade and Riyannah left the engineers to get on with their work. Blade ran the boarding party through a final series of exercises while Riyannah supervised the last stages of the clean-up.

A listening watch on the radio of the second shuttle detected no unusual or suspicious radio traffic. So far nobody seemed to have any idea that Station Four was in the underground's hands. That meant surprise was still with them. One of the engineers knew the appropriate codes and sent off periodic messages to make any listeners think Station Four was still alive, whole, and on the air.

This wouldn't fool the enemy forever, but it wouldn't have to. For another twelve hours after the shuttle took off, the underground fighters left behind would keep up appearances. Station Four would seem to be a busy part of Loyun Chard's space program, as far as anyone could tell from a distance. If any trucks or planes came in there

158

might be problems, but no shipments were scheduled for another three days. That would be plenty of time.

Twelve hours after the shuttle took off, the underground would evacuate the station, taking all the prisoners with them. Half an hour after that a series of explosions would completely demolish the station and thoroughly cover all signs of the night's battle.

Then the enemy wouldn't just suspect that something was wrong at Station Four. They'd know there had been an all-out attack by the underground, successful and devastating. They'd be too sure of this to inquire further, equally sure there could be no connection between the raid and the shuttle which flew up from Station Four twelve hours earlier. All their attention would be turned to tracking down the underground raiders.

This meant the underground people who stayed behind had nearly as dangerous a job as the boarding party. Their leader didn't seem to be worried. As he said to Blade:

"We've had too much practice dodging Chard's armed clowns to worry much. Even if they catch us, they'll find they've caught a pack of bat-cats. And if they do wipe us out—well, they'll be killing all their own people we've got as prisoners along with us. Even for Loyun Chard, soldiers and engineers don't grow on bushes."

Blade nodded. He was almost sorry he probably wouldn't be around to see the meeting between the leaders of the Targan underground and the War Council of Kanan. Meeting? He suspected that confrontation would be a better word.

Then it was time to load the shuttle. All twenty-five people in the boarding party changed into Targan Space Force coveralls and belted on Targan sidearms. Each one carried identification as a member of the staff or garrison of Station Four. The fake ID's wouldn't stand up under a real security check, so they'd still be better off if no one even knew they were aboard the starship. The coveralls and ID's were still a useful second line of defense, enough to deceive any casual observers.

Each person carried a standard Space Force flight bag, and in it a hurd-ray projector, hand grenades, and an explosive charge. They didn't have all their weapons and equipment on hand, but they had enough to do considerable damage to the starship and its crew. There was no way Loyun Chard could avoid a painful defeat now, unless the escort ships blew the shuttle and the boarding party out of the sky before they even reached *Dark Warrior*.

"That's unlikely," said Riyannah. "We know that they're expecting a shuttle from Station Four some time in the next few days. So why should they suspect this shuttle's a surprise package for them?" She grinned wickedly at the thought, baring teeth like a bat-cat about to bite.

Blade smiled. Watching Riyannah develop the instincts of a fighter and a battle leader was rewarding. He wondered if the Kananites would realize that she might be a better-than-average general if they needed one. He hoped the war wouldn't last that long, but if it did—why not General Riyannah?

The chief pilot broke into his thoughts. "All right, everybody. Two minutes to go. Strap in and relax." Shoulder and waist belts clicked into place and seats rattled back and forth as people adjusted them. Riyannah smiled. "No easy way out after this, is there?"

"No." Blade was glad she could smile about it. The boarding party was committed now, whatever happened. No easy retreat into the mountains or the forests for them, only a battle to the death. Twenty-five men and women, bearing the future of at least three worlds and perhaps more on their shoulders. Blade reached across to Riyannah and gripped her hand for a moment.

"One minute," said the pilot. Blade pulled his hand back and rested it loosely on the arm of his couch. He began breathing deeply to fill his system with oxygen for the high-g takeoff.

"Thirty seconds," said the pilot. Then it was twenty, after that ten, and after that:

"Nine—eight—seven—six—five—four—three—two—one—FIRING!"

The roar of the solid-fuel boosters hammered in through the soundproofed hull of the shuttle. Smoke blotted out the sky beyond the pilot's canopy. The shuttle vibrated, lurched, and lifted. A giant got both arms around Blade's chest and squeezed hard. He forced himself to go on breathing and keep his head still, remembering that the rockets only burned for thirty seconds.

Then the altimeter needle passed twenty thousand feet.

160

The rockets burned out and fell back toward the forest below. The roar was replaced by a faint hum as the anti-gravity cut in. Normal weight returned, and through the canopy Blade saw the sky turn from blue to purple. Then it turned black and the stars came out as the shuttle soared up into space.

Dark Warrior loomed in the shuttle's canopy, a fat cylinder slightly pointed at each end and covered with an eye-searing mirror finish to reflect laser beams. Blade stood between the two pilots, watching the starship grow steadily larger. No, "large" wasn't an adequate word to describe *Dark Warrior*. Neither was any other adjective that came to Blade's mind. Loyun Chard's starship was so huge it was hard to believe she'd even been built by human beings.

Blade had spent days with the ship's plans. He knew she was a mile long and a thousand feet in diameter amidships. He still found it hard to see a speck perched on the hull near the stern like a fly on a cow's rump and realize the speck was a hundred-foot shuttle like the one he rode.

Can twenty-five people really hope to do anything against that monster? Blade couldn't keep the thought out of his mind for a moment. He suspected that everyone else had exactly the same feeling. Then another thought replaced the first one.

Can twenty-five people be found in that monster if they're determined to hide? That was much more encouraging and made just as much sense. Part of that mile of steel was engine rooms and weapons bays, but there would still be enough space to swallow up ten boarding parties. Finding them would be rather like finding nests of mice in a twenty-room mansion when you didn't know what a mouse looked like.

Ten miles out, one of the escort ships challenged them. The pilots gave the shuttle's base and identification number and did not stop or slow down. One of the escorts flew formation with them for several minutes, then rejoined its comrades. Not one word of protest came over the radio.

Dark Warrior now stretched halfway across the sky ahead, blotting out a steadily growing number of stars. Another mile or two and they actually could ram her before the enemy could react. Security up here wasn't just

161

lax, it was practically nonexistent. The secret of Station Four was being well kept.

Four miles out, and the escort ship came back on the radio:

"Shuttle M 675, this is Green Patrol Leader. You are authorized to land and unload in Bay Two. Over."

"Acknowledged, Green Leader, and thank you. Over and out."

Three miles, two miles, one mile. There was no sky or stars left ahead, only the huge ship. The radio crackled again.

"Shuttle M 675, this is *Dark Warrior* Cargo Chief. We are illuminating Bay Two for you. Do you have your own cargo-handlers? We're a bit short-handed right now."

The pilot managed to keep a straight face as he replied, "M 675 to Cargo Chief. Yes, we've got our own people. Over and out." He cut off the radio, then he and Blade and Riyannah all laughed.

Now they were covering the last mile, and the starship became a vast wall of metal, both ends out of sight. A constellation of red and green lights winked to life around one of the hundred-foot square hatches amidships. The pilot made slight adjustments to the shuttle's course, then cut off its drive. Operating it within range of the starship's internal gravity field could burn out the generators.

The shuttle drifted in toward the hatch. The pilot pushed a button and a metal ring popped out of the nose. A jointed arm with a hook on the end reached out from one edge of the hatch and caught the ring. Blade gripped the back of the nearest couch as the cabin tilted around him. Slowly the shuttle was drawn down to the deck of Bay Two.

Chunnnnggg! The shuttle struck the deck and the arm lifted away. Jointed sections of deck folded themselves around the shuttle's belly, surrounding the hatches and sealing them off from the vacuum in the rest of Bay Two. Blade heard a rumble and a hissing as air was pumped into the newly-formed passageway. Then the radio came on again.

"Cargo Chief to M 675, you can start unloading at your convenience. Deposit cargo in Compartment 55GZ and leave the list on the door. One of my people will be around to pick it up later. Do you have any perishable cargo aboard?"

"None."

"All right. Get to work." The Cargo Chief's voice had the weary tones of a man who's worked long hours with little help and less pleasure. Blade had an image of the man sitting at a littered desk, red-eyed with fatigue, uniform rumpled, trying desperately to keep track of the cargoes pouring aboard *Dark Warrior*.

Blade pulled on a jacket over his coveralls and turned to the boarding party with a broad grin on his face. "All right, you people," he said, forcing a growl into his voice. "You heard the man. Get to work!"

Laughing, the boarding party began gathering up their equipment and pulling on their own jackets. Blade turned back to the pilots and looked up through the canopy. It gave him a good view of Bay Two, a steel box large enough to hold a fair-sized office building. In all that vast cavern he could see only one human figure, a spacesuited welder busily at work on the railing of a catwalk two hundred feet above Blade.

If the rest of *Dark Warrior* was as nearly deserted, the job of hiding and staying hidden might be almost easy.

Only two men passed by while the boarding party was unloading. Both were middle-aged, wearing rumpled coveralls and harried expressions. They looked like clerks, cooks, or something else equally uninspiring. They passed by without more than a casual glance at the boarding party.

In half an hour the shuttle was unloaded. All the legitimate cargo was properly stowed away in 55GZ, and all the other cargo was divided up into man-sized loads. Each member of the boarding party took up one load. Then Riyannah led them off to find a quiet hiding place among *Dark Warrior's* maze of empty cabins.

Blade, two of the engineers, and the two shuttle pilots stayed behind. Wishun, the senior engineer, was a grayhaired, stooped man with a perpetually sour expression. He'd lost his wife to Chard's Security people, but he'd retained his own status in the space program by publicly repudiating her. He'd done it for the sake of the underground, but the pain still showed in his face. The

163

other engineer, Draibo, was young, blond, bearded, and with an almost childlike enthusiasm for spaceflight and all that might come from it. He had no enthusiasm whatever for Loyun Chard.

Both engineers were scheduled to be part of the ship's flight crew, so their presence would make no one suspicious. The shuttle pilots were to stay until after Station Four was blown up, then wait to see how the enemy reacted. They were as respectable as the engineers and shouldn't be suspected of anything.

Blade was the only odd man out. He was the leader of the whole effort, not to mention the eyes, ears, and messenger for the hidden boarding party. He had to stay in the open, even at some risk. They'd minimized the risk by giving him a more complete set of fake ID's than the others. He was nominally a Sergeant-Major Kumish Dron, newly-appointed aide and bodyguard to the engineers. Both of them were senior enough to be allowed to bring staff members along with them, so no one was likely to question Blade's presence. He only hoped the other engineers, officers, and VIP's wouldn't do the same. Too many passengers and hangers-on could crowd even *Dark Warrior* enough to smoke the boarding party out of hiding.

The engineers were assigned quarters, then lay down to catch up on their sleep while Blade, like a good servant, unpacked their bags. The quarters were not as luxurious as the VIP suites, which rumor said had private steam baths and wine cellars, plush carpets and perfume dispensers in the air ducts. They were more than comfortable enough for the time they'd be needed.

Reckoning the time the shuttle landed aboard *Dark Warrior* as M, it was now M + 3 hours. Station Four should blow skyhigh at M + 8. If nobody changed plans because of that, *Dark Warrior* should be on her way no later than M + 80. Somewhere around M + 150 she should be within range of the asteroid base. Then the boarding party could come out of hiding and go to work.

It was going to be a long and tense week, but Blade was too experienced to let any amount of tension affect him seriously. He hoped the boarding party would be able to manage, enduring the same strain without the same experience.

Blade's mental diary of the next three days ran something like this:

M + 4—Blade went to sleep, to be reasonably fresh when the news broke about Station Four.

M + 7—Wishun and Draibo woke him up. Station Four was gone. Apparently the underground had to blow it prematurely. However, there was no sign that anyone suspected anything more than an unusually successful underground attack.

M + 9—It was officially confirmed over the ship's public address system: Station Four has been overrun and destroyed by the bandit underground. The enemy is being pursued and no quarter will be given. Meanwhile we of *Dark Warrior* must redouble our efforts, to bring vengeance to the memory of our comrades and glory to Loyun Chard and Targa.

M + 10—Blade set out to find Riyannah and the rest of the boarding party.

M + 13—Blade found what he was looking for. It was encouraging that the search took so long. The chances of anyone stumbling on the boarding party by accident appeared to be rather small.

The sheer size of *Dark Warrior* was impressive. So was the resources and technical ingenuity put into building her. If the ship hadn't been intended for such evil purposes, it would have been a pity to destroy. Even if she was destroyed and Chard overthrown, the Targans might very well go ahead and build another. They were going to be a force to reckon with in the future of this galaxy and this Dimension, whether the Kananites liked it or not.

Riyannah explained how she'd chosen the two cabins where the boarding party was hiding. "There's only one corridor approaching us, and we have that watched every minute. If somebody does come, we'll have plenty of time to retreat through the ventilation system. The ducts will easily take a fully-equipped man, and we've got a route all mapped out."

"Good work, General Riyannah," said Blade, and he wasn't entirely joking in calling her "General."

M + 14 through M + 50—Waiting, the monotony broken only by periodic reports of the pursuit of the "vile murderers of our comrades of Station Four." The "no quarter" slogan was a gruesome piece of good luck. If the enemy wasn't going to take any prisoners, they wouldn't be able to make any of the underground talk and reveal Plan Blade.

M + 52—*Dark Warrior's* captain decided that the homeless shuttle M 675 and her crew would be temporarily assigned to *Dark Warrior* and ride along with her. There was a moment of uncertainty for Blade—was the captain going to expect anyone beside the pilots to appear? Apparently not. Having the shuttle aboard meant the survivors of the boarding party, if any, wouldn't have to steal one of the ship's own lifeboats to escape after the battle.

M + 54—Three shuttles arrived in a bunch and started unloading black-uniformed State Security troops. They moved to quarters near the VIP suites. "It looks as if our passengers are going to join us a little early," said Wishun.

M + 60—It was announced that all crew for this mission should now be aboard and assigned quarters and duties. All hands had four hours to deal with personal matters and prepare for a formal review—full-dress uniform for armed forces personnel.

"We're not only getting our passengers early, it looks as if we're going to be on our way sooner than we expected," said Draibo.

"Do you really mind?" asked Blade.

"Hardly," said both engineers together. Every hour saved in getting out into space meant one less hour of waiting, one less hour with discovery and disaster possible.

M + 64—The engineers and the pilots headed for the wardroom, with Blade in his proper place behind them. By the time they got to the wardroom, it was packed with officers and their attendants. A good many of the officers were fully-armed State Security people, rather obviously keeping watch on everybody else. Blade was amused to note that the glowering State Security officers made the regular Targan officers much more nervous than they made him.

The ventilation system aboard *Dark Warrior* didn't have all the bugs out of it and the wardroom was packed almost wall to wall. It was already hot and stuffy and it was rapidly getting worse. Blade felt his face turning slimy with sweat and the high collar of his dress tunic sagging like a melting ice cream cone. No one else looked much more comfortable, even the State Security officers.

A whistle blew, then three trumpets sounded, ringing painfully in the closed metal compartment. Someone shouted, "Attention!" and Blade stiffened, right fist clenched on his chest in the formal Targan salute.

Then the main door of the wardroom opened and a man strode through. He was a large man, taller than Blade, and must have weighed close to three hundred pounds. Much of that weight was sheer fat, but he moved so fast and so smoothly that Blade knew there must be plenty of muscle still buried under the fat.

The man wore a pearl-gray uniform with blue trim, black leather boots, a gold mesh belt with a holstered laser pistol, and a high-peaked cap dripping with gold lace. On his chest were four rows of medals, with a pilot's wings perched in solitary splendor above them.

The face above the collar was the most arresting part of the man. Somehow the face had escaped its share of the man's fat. It was thickened, but the harsh lines of the jaw and mouth still showed clearly. The eyes were truly terrifying—large, blue, seeming to look everywhere at once without looking anywhere, the eyes of a man who saw everything and used everything he saw to his own advantage.

There was no doubt about it. This was a man where self-indulgence and cruelty were strong, but intelligence and ruthless ambition were even stronger. He would grab every bit of power Targa gave him, then reach out to the stars for more.

Blade would have guessed most of this about the man anyway, but he didn't have to guess. He'd seen too many pictures not to recognize Loyun Chard.

Chapter 22

Dark Warrior and her escorts were several hours out into space on the way to the asteroid before Blade could get back to the boarding party and tell them the news.

The Targans couldn't dance, sing, or cheer. There wasn't room to dance and singing or cheering might be overheard. In any case the expressions on their faces told Blade clearly enough what the new situation meant to them.

Having Loyun Chard himself aboard *Dark Warrior* opened the dazzling possibility of not just destroying the man's prize ship but of killing him outright. Like most tyrants he'd carefully avoided picking an heir, for fear the man might become ambitious to take over too soon. In fact he'd used the traditional tactics of playing off his various key supporters against one another. If Chard died aboard *Dark Warrior*, his supporters would immediately split into several suspicious and hostile factions. Each would control part of the armed forces, but none would have a decisive edge.

That of course would mean civil war on Targa, but for once the underground people didn't seem to care. Blade's major problem was persuading them not to storm the VIP quarters and try to kill Chard at once. That took another hour of desperate low-voiced argument. If Riyannah hadn't supported him, Blade might not have been able to win the argument.

"Blade and I want Chard's head as badly as you do," she said irritably. "Stop accusing us of being weak! It's just that we want to make sure we get it, not throw away our best chance by acting too soon.

"Consider. Right now we're only a few hours from Targa and there isn't a friendly warship within twenty million miles. The Security blackboys will have all their atten-

168

tion on guarding the leader and they outnumber us three to one.

"If we attack now, Chard can climb into one of the lifeboats and be safe aboard an escort ship long before we reach him. We'd lose our chance of getting him and maybe even our chance of crippling *Dark Warrior*. Then she certainly would be used for wiping out the underground's bases!

"If we stick to the original plan, we'll have a much better chance of getting both Chard and the ship. The Security men will be distracted by the fighting against the patrols. You've said yourself that they're more policemen and executioners than real soldiers or spacemen. We know Chard will be moving around, showing himself to his men as he always does. We may be able to ambush him. Even if he does get off *Dark Warrior*, there will be Kananite and Menel ships all around us. They may pick him off if we can't."

The argument wavered back and forth for a while longer, but eventually the Targans agreed that Blade and Riyannah were right. Plan Blade would go forward on schedule.

Outside in the corridor, Blade whispered to Riyannah, "Actually I think the engineers, the pilots, and I are the people with the best hopes of getting the bastard. We've got the freedom to move around and the chance to learn his movements. We'll also have the best chance to strike by surprise."

"Five of you against Chard and all his guards?"

"Three, actually. The pilots ought to stay out of the fighting as much as possible and be ready to take us off."

"Three people." Riyannah sighed. "Do you think you have any chance?"

"Of killing Chard, yes. Of getting out afterward—" He shrugged. "I don't know. And I don't like it any better than you do. But we've got to get Chard."

"You think I don't know that?" said Riyannah almost angrily. "I just wish— Oh, I wish a lot of things that aren't possible." She kissed him. "Good luck and don't get killed if you don't have to."

Blade returned to his quarters and sat down with Wishun and Draibo to lay plans. *Dark Warrior* moved steadily out into space.

169

Sixty hours out from Targa, the annoucement came.

"All hands—general call to Battle Stations in five hours."

Blade caught a quick meal in the nearest NCO's mess. The two pilots slipped away to join the boarding party. The two engineers stayed in their cabin, too tense to eat. They weren't veterans at this sort of thing, and Blade himself found he had to get the food down a mouthful at a time. He'd never before faced a battle where he had so great a chance of doing something important or so small a chance of coming out in one piece.

He still went through his preparations with his usual grim professional care. He'd modified a uniform jacket with hidden pouches. Now he dropped four of the small blue grenades into one pouch. Into another he dropped a canister of Targan riot-control gas. It produced violent sneezing, severe nausea, and temporary blindness.

In the last pouch he put a small hurd-ray pistol with an oversized power cell. He planned to use it on the maximum overload setting. This would use up even a Kananite power cell in a couple of minutes, but it would also produce a lethal beam. Loyun Chard and anyone else who got in its way would be not only dead but disintegrated into smoking chunks.

Then Blade hung his well-armed jacket on the foot of his bed, lay down, and went to sleep.

Someone was shaking him. Blade woke up and swung his feet to the floor before he recognized who it was. Wishun was standing by the bed.

"They've just called Battle Stations," he said. "Time we were moving." His face was very pale, but his hands were steady as he pulled on his own jacket.

"Any reports of attacking ships?" Blade asked.

"None so far. Do you think—the enemy—have changed their plans?" They called the defenders of the asteroid base "the enemy" to confuse any possible eavesdroppers.

"They had no way of getting word to us, but I doubt it," said Blade. "They haven't got many choices." He stood up. "Let's go."

The plan was simple enough, and even gave them a small chance of getting clear afterward. Its timing, though, was at the mercy of Chard's movements. They had to

170

strike while he was in or near the Battle Command Center, watching the opening stages of the attack on the asteroid. That meant they might not be able to synchronize their attack with the boarding party's. It was a risk, but one Blade was willing to run for a chance to kill Chard.

The corridor to the elevator they were using was nearly empty. Even with nearly four hundred men aboard and most of them on the move, *Dark Warrior* seemed half-deserted. Blade mentally crossed his fingers, hoping the boarding party could hide for another hour. If they could, there was no way Loyun Chard could escape a stinging defeat.

Damn it, he didn't just want Chard defeated now! He wanted the man dead! Blade pulled his face into an impassive mask and followed the two engineers into the elevator.

The elevator let them out on the Command Deck. There was a guard post at the entrance to the circular corridor around the Battle Command Center. Blade and the engineers were offering their ID's to the Security man on duty when a gong began sounding urgently.

"Attention, all hands. Two squadrons of enemy ships are approaching. The escorts are preparing to engage, but they will be within range of us before long. Vengeance for our comrades of Station Four! Glory to our Leader Chard!"

All Blade's senses were now as alert as a hunting animal's. The approach of ships from the asteroid base would certainly get the boarding party moving if it was still in hiding. The alarm might be up within minutes and then Loyun Chard would be on the move also, perhaps moving out of their reach. He and the engineers might have to take the first opportunity they had to strike.

Blade took his ID back from the guard and followed the engineers into the corridor beyond the guard post. It formed a circle a hundred and fifty feet in diameter. Opening off the inner side were six large rooms holding computers and other supporting equipment. In the very center of the circle was the Battle Command Center, fifty feet across and two decks high. Wishun's battle station was in Computer Room One, which also had the main entrance to the BCC. If Chard had to leave in a hurry, he would most likely be coming right past Wishun and Blade.

171

Draibo turned off into Fire Control Two, his station. He was supposed to stay there for ten minutes or until he heard firing. If he didn't hear any firing, he was to come over to Computer One and start a brawl with Wishun. From there on things would develop rapidly, and they all hoped successfully.

Computer One reminded Blade somewhat of the main computer room in the Project's underground complex. Even the finish on the computer consoles was gray and faintly crackled. Nothing was really missing except the sullen gray rock of the walls and Lord Leighton bustling about in his filthy old laboratory coat.

There was nothing to do for an engineer's aide when the ship was at Battle Stations except run errands, and there were no errands to run. Blade pulled a folding seat out of the wall and sat down, trying to look both military and inconspicuous at the same time. He didn't need to try very hard. Everyone in the room was too busy to pay any attention to him.

They were all hunched over their consoles, sweaty faces turned to the rainbow displays of lights, hands dancing over knobs, switches, and keyboards. A screen over one console showed a pit of black space with a distant powdering of stars and a few larger specks darting and wheeling. Twice explosions flared among the specks, but Blade couldn't tell if anyone was getting hit. *Dark Warrior's* own lasers and missiles didn't seem to be in action yet. The loudspeakers were pouring out a continuous stream of announcements about enemy ships being engaged and vengeance for the dead of Station Four. There would be vengeance before long, but not for any of Loyun Chard's men.

Blade flexed his shoulders to loosen cramped muscles and felt the reassuring weight of the weapons concealed inside his jacket. He unzipped the jacket a few more inches so he could reach inside for a quick draw with the hurd-ray.

Faint and far off, something went *whummmp*. Blade heard it through the air, felt the vibration through the deck, and stiffened. Several men raised their heads from consoles to look around uncertainly. Another fainter *whummmp* came. Blade's eyes met Wishun's. He forced himself to keep his hands resting in his lap.

172

Blade's watch showed nine minutes since he'd sat down. In another minute Draibo should appear and—

The loudspeaker gave off a high-pitched whistle. Everyone in the room stiffened along with Blade and the Security guards reached for their pistols. "Attention, attention, all hands!" came the urgent voice. "Emergency! Armed agents of the traitors are aboard. Stand by your posts, do your duty, and defend our Leader with your lives!"

Then the door to the corridor opened and Draibo strode through, mouth open, eyes wide and staring at Wishun, hands dangling at his side but twisted into claws. Blade rose, a guard turned toward the young engineer, and then the door to the Battle Command Center slid open and Loyun Chard stepped through.

There was a solid mass of black uniforms behind the leader but only two Security men beside him. Blade knew he'd never have a better chance. With one hand he drew the hurd-ray and with the other plucked out a grenade. One of the men flanking Chard saw Blade move but did the wrong thing in response. Instead of drawing and firing, he gallantly threw himself in front of his leader, opening his mouth to shout a warning. He died with his mouth open as Blade's hurd-ray tore the whole upper part of his body into smoking pieces.

The remains of the body thudded to the deck, giving Blade a clear shot at Loyun Chard. The leader was reeling backward, face blackened, eyes shut, uniform smouldering, charred lips peeled back from his teeth. His three hundred pounds crashed into the guards behind him. Some of them went down, others were blocked by their leader's massive body, the rest were too stunned to react. Blade aimed at Chard's head and fired again. The head vanished in a cloud of smoke. Guards behind the toppling Chard screamed as Blade kept the trigger pressed down and the hurd-ray pouring into their ranks. Suddenly the doorway to the Battle Command Center was clear. Blade shifted his aim to the second of Chard's flanking guards, burning through the man's chest. With the other hand he hurled the grenade through the doorway.

It went off with a resounding metallic crash and the concussion made Blade's ears ring. In the confined space of the Battle Command Center he suspected the one grenade would be enough to flatten everybody. He threw a second, just to make sure everyone there would be not only down but out. Then he signaled to Wishun and Draibo. They'd drawn their own hurd-rays and were covering their fellow engineers and technicians. None of them looked ready to join in the fight and most of them looked as if they'd much rather be several light-years away.

Wishun fired a blast into the smoke-fogged door of the Battle Command Center, then turned to the men at the consoles. "Good luck at coming through this day. Targa will need your services even though Chard's gone. You may have a chance to redeem yourself for serving him." He looked at Chard's headless corpse as if he'd like to spit on it, then turned away to follow Blade out into the corridor.

A wild burst of firing greeted them as they reached the guard post. The guards were gone but Blade saw a cluster of Security men on the far side of the room, near the elevator doors. They seemed to be firing wildly at anything that moved. Blade and the engineers went to cover behind the guard post's console and opened fire. Thirty seconds' work with the hurd-rays turned the Security men into a heap of corpses. Blade led the others toward the elevator. He hoped it was still working. They had to get far from the Command Deck as soon as possible.

A laser beam went *pfffht*. Wishun staggered, clawing at his chest. Then he fired at the wounded Security man until the laser pistol and the arm holding it were both ashes. Blade gripped Wishun by one arm and pulled him toward the elevator.

"No," the engineer gasped. "It's through the lung. I'm not going to make it out of here. Give me a grenade so I can do a little more damage. Then run!"

"Wishun—" began Draibo, but the older man shook off Blade's grip with desperate strength.

"No, damn you!" he snarled, then coughed. When he'd finished coughing there was blood on his lips and trickling down his chin. Silently Blade gave him the grenade. Then he and Draibo scrambled into the nearest elevator car and punched for the farthest level they could find on the control panel.

The car was four levels down when they heard the grenade explode. They looked at each other but there was nothing to be said. Wishun was gone to join his wife and the rest of Chard's victims, knowing that he'd helped defeat their murderer. If a man had to die violently at all, there were many worse ways to go.

The elevator took Blade and Draibo all the way down to the end of its shaft. It let them out in a low, dimly-lit, and completely deserted corridor. From beyond an armored door across the corridor came the sound of machinery. The color coding on the door showed that it led to an ammunition handling room. While Draibo watched the corridor, Blade punched the control button for the door. As it whined open, he tossed a grenade through the gap, then jumped aside.

The grenade must have connected with something else explosive, because the blast nearly blew the door out of its frame. Ignoring the new ringing in his ears, Blade stepped inside and played the hurd-ray over every visible piece of machinery and human body. By the time he'd finished, the room was a stinking shambles that would never handle ammunition again. Coughing fiercely, he backed out into the corridor again and gathered up Draibo.

How long he and the engineer roamed through the corridors of *Dark Warrior*, Blade never knew. They lost all sense of time and sometimes nearly all sense of direction. Without *Dark Warrior's* immense size, the boarding party could never have hidden themselves aboard her or launched their attack. That same size also made getting places a slow process and getting completely lost a fairly easy one. At times all Blade and Draibo could do was keep moving and keep shooting, hoping they'd come out somewhere. In the meantime, they'd stay alive and do as much damage as they could.

Their own weapons were quickly exhausted and they had to rely on lasers and rifles captured from the enemy. Both of them had minor burns and bullet grazes in half a dozen places, their faces were blackened, their clothes frayed. Draibo cracked a bone in his right wrist diving for cover and after that had to shoot left-handed.

They kept on, although it was impossible to know how the rest of the battle was going. *Dark Warrior's* own heavy weapons were in action, for they could feel and hear them. She was also taking hits from the Kananite and Menel ships, heavy enough to jolt even her huge mass.

175

The lights, ventilation, and elevators were still running, so the life support and internal power systems hadn't taken any vital damage. The public address system was also still alive, but the few announcements coming over it were either uninformative or completely incoherent. The situation aboard *Dark Warrior* was simply developing too fast for her surviving officers to keep track of it.

At last the public address system went off the air in a chorus of screams, explosions, and static. It never came back on. Minutes later Blade and Draibo, more blackened and battered than ever, burst into the fire control room for Laser Bank Seven.

The five men there were professionals. Blade had to give them credit for that. They were still shooting accurately as Blade and Draibo entered, even though four of their six laser tubes were out of action. Even with bullets whistling about their ears the two men at the main control panel still managed to put a beam into a Menel patrol ship. It limped off, trailing smoke, then blazed up like a miniature nova and became a cloud of bluish gas.

By the time the explosion died, the five men of Bank Seven were all down, sprawled on the bloody decks or slumped over their controls, heads smashed in by Blade's rifle butt. Draibo was also down, with half a dozen slugs in his belly. He was smiling, because he knew they'd won and also because he knew he'd be dead before the shock wore off and his wounds started hurting. Blade propped him up so he could see the undamaged screen. For a minute or two they both watched the battle in space around *Dark Warrior*.

By now it must have been going on for hours, but it was still as savage as ever. It was impossible to tell who was winning the ship-to-ship combat. *Dark Warrior's* escorts had the edge in firepower but they were outnumbered three or four to one. Blade stepped up the magnification on the screen, hoping to see more than darting specks and lines of fire.

A familiar streamlined wedge shape drifted into view— *Trenbar*, closely engaged with a Targan ship. *Trenbar* seemed to be half-crippled, maneuvering slowly and erratically as the enemy closed. The Targans were pouring laser fire into what they thought was a nearly helpless target when *Trenbar* suddenly came to life again. Whipping

176

around in a high-g turn, she plunged straight at the enemy. A laser scored her side and peeled away a chunk of armor but didn't turn her aside. The two ships merged, then both were blotted out in an expanding ball of purple flame.

Before Blade's eyes recovered from the glare, he heard a sharp metallic *whannnngggg* and the floor quivered under his feet. Several more impact noises came in the next few seconds, followed by the unmistakable hiss of escaping air. Blade realized what was happening. *Trenbar* had fought her last battle so close to *Dark Warrior* that fragments from the explosion were hitting the starship like meteors, tearing through even her hull. It was time to be moving on again.

Draibo was dead, a smile fading from his bloody lips. Blade saluted him, then saluted the screen where the gas cloud was vanishing. Then he twisted the power setting on the remaining lasers to OVERLOAD and switched them on. When the explosion came, that would be the end of Laser Bank Seven and every Targan within fifty feet of it.

The air in the room was definitely getting thin, and Blade could see smoke creeping toward one section of wall. Nothing more to do here. He ran out, closing the door behind him and fusing the lock with a laser burst. Even out in the corridor the air was thinner and the light was dimmer. Time to head for Bay Two if he didn't want to risk being trapped aboard a dying ship.

Blade took a deep breath, then broke into a run.

Blade ran along *Dark Warrior's* corridors and down her stairs and ladders as he'd seldom run before in his life. He saw a few Targans, but half of them were dead or dying and he went past the rest so fast they had no time to fire. Most of the great ship seemed to be deserted. Was the crew dead, preoccupied with damage control, or abandoning ship? Blade didn't know. Certainly the ship herself was dying, and Blade knew he was in a race with time to keep from dying with her.

Laser Bank Seven exploded, knocking Blade off his feet. Ignoring new bruises he picked himself up and ran on. The main lighting went out, but the emergency lighting came on, leaving the corridors in a sinister twilight. The elevators went out and so did the power for opening the doors. Blade had to open each one manually, releasing

177

latches and twisting wheels with blistered, sweating hands. He didn't bother closing doors behind him anymore, even though escaping air was now making a noticeable draft everywhere. He didn't have the time to be neat, and in any case the more air that leaked out the better. Even if *Dark Warrior* couldn't be destroyed outright, she could still be reduced to an airless hulk.

Blade reached the entrance to Bay Two just as the ship's internal gravity field died. The door stood open and several bodies lay on the deck around it. Most were ship's crew, but Blade recognized two of the boarding party. As the gravity went off, the bodies floated up from the deck. Blade brushed past him and pulled himself through the door.

A hundred feet away an undamaged shuttle M 675 was floating just clear of the deck. She was turning slowly as the pilot used the altitude control jets to line her up with the outer hatch. Blade fired a burst from his rifle to attract attention, then threw his rifle away and launched himself across the bay like a slow-motion rocket.

They saw him coming. The belly hatch slid open and a weighted line shot out toward him. Blade twisted in mid-air, caught the line with his fingertips, and held on by sheer willpower until it pulled him to a stop. Then he took a more secure grip and let himself be drawn inside the shuttle.

The hatch slammed shut so fast Blade barely got his feet out of the way in time. Riyannah kissed him, then shoved a face-covering mask with an oxygen bottle attached at him.

"We're going to have to ram through the outer hatch," she shouted. "Put this on, quick!" Blade pulled on the mask and shot up the ladder to the main cabin on Riyannah's heels.

There was only one pilot at the controls now and only twelve of the boarding party in their seats. Some of them were wounded and all of them were as ragged and dirty as Blade himself, but all of them cheered wildly as he appeared.

The pilot shoved his mask up and looked at Blade. "I was all ready to assume you were dead," he said, grinning. "But she threatened to blow my head off if I left before you appeared and the others agreed with her. So what could I do?" The grin faded. "Get to a couch and hang on. We're going to have to go right through the outer doors and it's going to be rough." He turned back to the controls, pulling his mask on as Blade dove for the nearest couch.

He'd barely got himself strapped in when the pilot cut in the shuttle's own drive. With the drive wide open the shuttle could accelerate to several hundred miles an hour inside Bay Two, and also flatten everyone aboard into their couches. Blade felt as if a whole family of elephants was sitting on his chest. Then a horrible screech of tearing metal half-deafened him. He was jolted and jerked about as if one of the elephants had picked him up in its trunk and tossed him high in the air. More metal screeched, the canopy cracked in half a dozen places, and then there was space and stars ahead.

The shuttle raced away from *Dark Warrior* under full power, relying on speed rather than maneuvering for safety. As *Dark Warrior* faded behind them, the pilot turned to his passengers and pushed up his mask.

"There's some transparent tape in Locker K. One of you get it out and slap some on the canopy. The main cabin's still tight but keep your masks on anyway. We may still get shot at a bit before we're out of this."

Blade unbuckled himself, floated over to Locker K, and dug out the roll of heavy glassy tape. He was just floating up past the pilot when suddenly there was a new sun in the sky. It swelled up, poured out light for a minute that seemed like an hour, then faded.

Dark Warrior was gone.

Riyannah drifted up beside Blade as the light from the exploding starship died. "We put one bomb in the main power supply and rigged a warhead in the missile magazine. We would have been perfectly happy to just cripple the ship, then take her as a prize, but—" She shrugged.

Blade held her hand. "I know. It would have been a fine ending to our victory. We could have learned a good deal more about the Targans from examining *Dark Warrior*. But it doesn't matter now. The ship's gone and so is Loyun Chard. Anything else the Targans do in space for a long time to come will be peaceful."

"We hope," said Riyannah softly.

"It's mostly up to you Kananites," said Blade. "The

179

Targans will be just as proud without Loyun Chard as they were under him. I suspect the Menel will also have—"

As if mentioning the Menel had called them, the radio came to life. Blade recognized the voice coming across space as the Speaker-translated Menel ambassador.

"Targan shuttle, do you have Richard Blade aboard?"

Blade took the microphone. "I'm aboard."

"Well done, and so say all of us who fought in this battle. It is your victory. Do you wish to be picked up?"

Blade looked at the pilot, who nodded. "Yes. This shuttle's taken a bit of a beating."

"Very good. Stay on your present course and we will rendezvous within fifteen minutes." Silence.

Blade finished taping up the cracks in the canopy, then drifted down into the cabin, hand in hand with Riyannah. They perched on the arms of couches side by side and looked at each other in silence. They were both drained to limp rags by the strain of the fight, too drained to think of anything worth saying out loud.

The minutes crept by. The pilot was just reporting the Menel ambassador's ship on the radar screen, when Blade felt a familiar pain stab through his head. He rose from the couch, floating upward as he tore off his mask. Riyannah stared up at him.

"Are you going Home?"

The pains were coming harder and faster than usual, but Blade managed to get out a strangled "Yes." He thought, *This is the first time I've been able to tell someone in Dimension X where I'm going. I'm glad it's Riyannah I can tell.* "Good-bye and good luck," he gasped. Then the pain was so fierce he could no longer think or speak. He reached out, felt Riyannah's fingers on his arm, then felt them slip down and pat the bracelet on his wrist. His own fingers twisted, clutching at hers, holding on.

The touch of Riyannah's fingers on his was the last thing Blade remembered as the pain in his head blotted out everything.

Chapter 23

Blade walked along the sands of Dover Beach, listened to the rumble of the surf on the shore, and looked up at the stars.

He didn't look at them with any hope they'd help him sort out his thoughts. He'd already done that, as much as he ever could. He thought he'd done rather well, considering what an absolutely cosmic can of worms this last mission to Dimension X had opened! He'd thought his meeting with the Wizard of Rentoro would hold the record for confusion and complication for a while, but here was the very next trip and the record was up in smoke!

At least Lord Leighton had rolled with the punch and come up swinging. Instead of dying of frustration over all the maddening new questions this trip posed, he was behaving like a small boy let loose in a candy store with a five-pound note.

"You've opened up a whole new approach to Dimension X and all the related phenomena," he'd said, practically rubbing his hands in glee. "We badly need to explore the possibility of movement through space during the transition into Dimension X. I've always said so but I've never been able to get any support from the people who control the appropriations. Fantasy, they call it. Nonsense! I knew I was right, and now they'll have to admit it and provide an appropriation for exploring the possibilities."

J's eyebrows rose. He'd heard Lord Leighton conjure up the need for more appropriations often enough before. If all Leighton's brainstorms were added up, the total bill for Project Dimension X would resemble the annual appropriations for the Royal Air Force.

"How much do you expect to need for this exploration?"

181

"For the preliminary stages, no more than a million pounds or so. We'll have to—" Here Leighton went off into a long list of people and equipment that would be needed, most of which was Greek to Blade.

J's eyebrows rose higher as Leighton went on. When the scientist paused for breath, he asked quietly, "How much do you expect to need eventually?"

Leighton shot the other man a sharp, suspicious glance. He knew exactly why J was asking this question, but still wouldn't be held back from answering it. "A minimum of ten million pounds over the next five to six years."

That more or less ended the discussion for the time being. No doubt Leighton would get some extra money to start off in this new direction. It was far too important to be ignored entirely. But ten million pounds! Blade could see J trying hard not to laugh as they left Leighton's office.

Here on Dover Beach, Blade did laugh. Leighton certainly had something worth exploring. The computer had snatched Blade back across a hundred million miles of space as well as across the Dimensions. Perhaps they *were* on the edge of discovering a method of teleportation.

Yet Blade had to wonder. Was Lord Leighton perhaps dashing off after the possibility of teleportation so he would not have to face the infinity of infinities the Menel scientist had suggested, and what it might mean for not only the Project but for all science? Lord Leighton's intellect was immensely powerful and his courage undoubted—but were there things before which even he quailed? It was a question Blade knew he would never get out of his mind, or ever be able to answer.

So Blade preferred to leave the possibilities and perhapses of science to Lord Leighton. His mind turned back to remember the other, more solid things he'd done on this trip.

The techincal films made the trip back with him, slightly fogged by radiation in some places but mostly legible. The solar collectors would take some time to develop, because they depended on combinations of metals that apparently were much more common on Kanan than on Earth. The power cells, on the other hand, were something that could be in mass production within a few years. His trip had probably put forward the arrival of a practical electric automobile by a decade or more.

182

What had he left behind? He'd left Riyannah—and as he thought of her he looked at the glowing bracelet on his wrist. He'd left her, but if there'd been any way to do it otherwise— No, he hadn't loved Riyannah—he hadn't allowed himself to love her, although it was certain she'd loved him.

It was also certain that if he ever found in Home Dimension a woman with her qualities, he would love her and leave no stone unturned to marry her. She might not enjoy the ordeal of seeing him hurled off to Dimension X time after time, but she could endure it, and between trips there would be so much they could share.

So he'd left Riyannah—left her in a strong position to influence Kananite policy. He'd left the whole of Kanan shaken to the point where they'd have to look for new ways of dealing with other races. He'd left Loyun Chard dead, his starship destroyed, his regime crippled, and his enemies greatly strengthened. The Targan underground might not win easily, but no one would be able to ignore them now—and that included the Kananites as well as their fellow Targans.

He'd brought home a treasure of the stars, but he'd also left much behind in payment.

★★★★★★★★★★★★★★★★★★★★★★★★★★★★★★★★★★

BLADE

by Jeffrey Lord

Richard Blade is Everyman, a mighty and intrepid hero exploring the hitherto-uncharted realm of worlds beyond our knowledge, in the best tradition of America's most popular heroic fantasy giants such as Tarzan, Doc Savage, and Conan.

| Over 2 million copies sold! |